LOSING Stars

THE CELEBRITY SERIES, BOOK #3

Quinn & Ryson

by

J. Sterling

THE LUCKIEST GIRL

Quinn

"**R**YSONNNN!" I SHOUTED at the top of my lungs from the depths of our master bathroom, knowing full well that he wouldn't be able to hear me.

It wasn't that our house in Malibu was insanely large as much as it was that our bedroom was at the very far end, and if you were anywhere else in the house, you might as well have been on a different block.

I waited a few seconds for a response, and when none came, I rushed over and pressed the intercom button. "Ryson?"

After months of not being able to hear each other if one of us was in the bedroom, we decided to put in an intercom system. I'd fought against it at first, feeling like it was far too pretentious, but it was one of my favorite features now. No matter where Ryson was in the house, he couldn't escape me. One press of the button, and he was at my whim. I loved this damn intercom.

"What's up, babe?" he responded immediately.

"Can you come here, please? It's a fashion emergency."

I heard him laugh before the intercom crackled, and the sound of his footsteps pounding against the wood floor in the distance quickly grew louder with his approach.

"Your knight in shining armor is here, milady."

Turning around slowly, I lifted my long blonde hair from my back. "Can you zip me up, please?"

"This is your emergency?" He chuckled. When I didn't respond, his lips found their way to my exposed skin, and his fingers ran down my spine. "I'd rather unzip you."

"I know you would, but they'll be here any second." I tried to swat at his shoulder but failed as he twisted out of my reach.

His fingertips grazed up my back as the zipper followed. Slowly. Seductively. "You look beautiful," he said as his fingers came to an abrupt stop.

I turned around to face him, my cheeks flushed with warmth from his touch. Even after all this time, Ryson still got to me, still made me feel like I was a teenager all over again. "Thank you."

"Anything for you." He leaned down and placed a sweet kiss on my lips, and my body instinctively pressed up against his, his hands holding me tightly in place.

"I love you," I said as I looked into his dark brown eyes. Eyes that I had memorized, every fleck of color etched into my brain.

"And I love you," he said back, and I held my breath, waiting for his next words. I knew they'd come. "Forever." He kissed me once more, and I relaxed against him. "Forever, Quinn," he reinforced, breaking the kiss.

"And then some." I smiled softly as the doorbell rang.

Ryson placed a final kiss on my forehead. "I'll go get it. You look amazing, babe."

"Thank you. I'll be out in a second." I turned around and faced the mirror one last time, running my hands down the length of my multicolored sundress.

Ryson and I had been inseparable since the night he showed up at my trailer on set after a tumultuous year.

My parents had been concerned at first, fearing that we were far too young to be so serious. They were convinced that he was going to not only break my heart, but also decimate it. But after a year and a half of dating, they admitted to me that they'd never met anyone quite like Ryson and that if he was the one for me, they understood and fully supported us. They said it was the way he looked at me; like I'd hung the moon, the way he treated me, the way he talked to me, and the way he loved me. Both of my parents had claimed they'd never seen anything like it and that love was love, no matter when we first found it.

It wouldn't have mattered anyway. To be fair, it would have haunted me if my parents hadn't approved of Ryson, but it wouldn't have stopped me from being with him. He was a risk worth taking, a challenge worth accepting, a battle worth fighting. That boy had loved me with a ferocity I was certain no one else ever would. And he loved me even harder now that he was a man. I was the luckiest woman on the planet, and I damn well knew it.

The sound of voices drifted my way, but I couldn't tell if it was my actress and best friend Paige and her boyfriend,

Tatum, or if it was our other close friends, rock-god-turned-actor Walker Rhodes and his talent agent girlfriend, Madison. It didn't matter as I finalized highlighting my cheeks and scooted out of the bathroom.

With all six of our lives being intertwined the way that they were, I'd had the idea to host a dinner party for a more intimate gathering. Every time we all got together, it was usually for an industry event, and while we mingled and networked, we rarely saw each other one-on-one. I'd decided that we didn't get to spend enough quality time together. Thankfully, they'd all agreed. Or maybe they simply knew better than to disagree with me. I wouldn't have let up until I got my way, and they all knew it.

Speed-walking down my hallway, I smiled as I rounded the corner and locked eyes with Madison Myers, wrapped in her rock-star boyfriend's arms. Madison was one of Hollywood's most exclusive up-and-coming agents. She'd quickly garnered a stellar reputation for actually caring about her clients' well-being instead of the money she could make, and she was extremely particular about who she signed on to represent—hence the clamoring by everyone in LA to be represented by her. Not only was she good at her job, but she was also Walker Rhodes's girlfriend. Walker was an international singing sensation, who had made the leap into movies with her help and guidance. He was now well on his way to becoming as big of a star on the screen as he was off.

Personally, I enjoyed Madison as a person. The fact that she was smart and mouthy was a bonus in my eyes. I admired strength and integrity, and she was the epitome of both.

"Hey, Mads. You look beautiful." I enveloped her in a hug, admiring her shorts and vintage bohemian top.

"Uh, you do too. I suddenly feel underdressed," she said with a laugh, waving a hand in my direction.

"It's just a sundress. You look great!"

Her face screwed up before she blurted out, "Maybe it's just your stupid face. It's always perfect and pretty, and I hate you."

I laughed as I squeezed her again. "I love this girl, Walker. She's good people." I turned toward Walker Rhodes and his handsomely tanned face.

He hugged me and planted a kiss on my cheek. "Eh, she's all right." He shrugged, and I socked him in the shoulder.

Two quick knocks rapped on the door before it opened, and my best friend, Paige, and her hot-as-hell Southern boyfriend, Tatum, walked through.

Paige Lockwood had been my best friend since we met on the set of her first movie when we were both teenagers. She was terrified and looked like she was about to throw up until I gave her some of my food. If Paige had been any other actress on the planet, our relationship would have most likely ended there. But Paige was unlike anyone I'd ever met before; she was naive, kind, and genuine. There wasn't an ounce of connivance or a malicious bone in her body, and I had instantly been drawn to those parts of her, recognizing how rare they were. We never competed with each other— not for boys, not for roles, not for anything.

Not too long ago, Paige had had a mini meltdown and run

away from home. That was what I liked to call it anyway. She ran—drove—away and ended up meeting this ridiculously hot and talented guy named Tatum in Middle of Nowhere, Louisiana. After a bunch of drama, pure Hollywood-style, Tatum ended up moving to LA to be with Paige. He'd also landed a job writing music for Walker—which, for the record, he'd earned even though he could have anything handed to him at this point. Being Paige's boyfriend came with serious perks.

Walking past Paige, I headed straight for Tatum's open arms. "Love muffin," I proclaimed for everyone to hear as I snuggled against his chest, a joke we'd started soon after he moved here.

"Pretty bird," he responded, petting my hair.

Paige pretended to puke. "This love affair is annoying," she whined before sauntering over to Ryson and wrapping herself in my boyfriend's arms.

"I can't even be mad. I love him too," Ryson said before kissing Paige on the side of the head and walking toward me and Tatum. Shoving me out of the way, he gave Tatum a man hug, and I pretended to struggle for balance.

If any two guys had a bromance going on, it was those two. They had bonded instantly upon meeting even though Ryson should have hated him—or at least given him the fifth degree for allowing Paige to believe that he didn't care about her. It was all a defense mechanism on Tatum's part, but still. Ryson had practically fallen in love with him on the spot. It was disgusting. And I loved everything about it.

"I feel sort of left out," Walker complained.

"It's just that you're old news, bud. He's newer," Ryson said with a laugh before waving Walker over.

The three of us girls watched them behave like little boys, high-fiving and giving one another slaps on the backs. All the while, we secretly enjoyed every second of their antics. We knew how blessed we were.

"It's cute how much they love each other," Paige said.

"I know. I sort of love it," Madison agreed, and I nodded.

"I'm more happy that I love both of you. Screw them. What if *we* hated each other?" I asked in mock horror.

"We're the only reason there is a *them*," Paige added as she pointed between the three of us girls.

"True. Good point," I said with a smile. "This whole college thing is making you smart."

Paige had decided to go to college this past year, so she could go through the kinds of things that people our age were experiencing. It had taken one hell of a fight for her to get there, but she was in a much better place now. After her runaway meltdown, she'd fired her old agent and hired our friend Madison, and I'd never seen her happier.

"I love college," she all but cooed, and I fought off the urge to roll my eyes at her.

Unlike Paige, I had zero desire for her sense of normalcy. We had agreed it was because I'd been acting since birth and Paige had been plucked from her family and friends during her teenage years. Being ripped away from everyone like that had made her feel like she was always missing out on the things her friends were doing and posting about on social media. Personally, I'd never wanted to be anywhere but where I was—in the public eye, acting. I didn't know any different, and I wasn't looking for it either.

Everything that truly made me happy was standing in my living room.

My eyes met Ryson's, and he gave me a wink. My insides heated. I hoped I'd always feel about him the way I did today.

EXCITABLE FUTURES
Quinn

A FTER DINNER AND a few too many drinks, Ryson started getting overly excited about his latest project idea as we all sat at the dining room table, listening raptly.

Ryson had done time in rehab after we first met. His brief vice with drugs could have ruined his life, but after rehab, he never touched them again, and as far as I knew, he wasn't ever even tempted. It'd turned out that he didn't have an addictive personality the way he had feared, and the drugs had merely been something that, once he started, he wasn't able to quit on his own without help. Even though the rehab experts had highly advised Ryson to quit all substances forever, fearing a relapse, we both drank socially, and so far, it had never been an issue.

Ryson coughed, waved a hand in the air to quiet us all down, and shouted, "No, really. Listen to me," as we all continued to focus on him. "I'm not joking. Quinn and I are doing it, and I think you all should consider it too."

"Wait, what are we doing?" I joked toward the opposite end of the table, where the love of my life sat, as my drink splashed onto my fingers.

"The reality show." He shrugged, and everyone looked between us. "Right, babe? You liked the idea when we talked about it before, didn't you?" He sounded so unsure when, only two seconds ago, he'd declared it to the entire table with pride and confidence.

I smiled at him. "Yes, babe. I loved the idea," I agreed. Then, I continued before I could stop myself, "I'd like it even more if you proposed to me during it." I slapped a hand over my mouth as if my own words had surprised me. They hadn't. I was obsessed with marrying Ryson in the same way that he was obsessed with never getting married.

It was our one obstacle. And it felt almost insurmountable at times.

His parents' failed relationship had completely soured him to the idea. He told me that exchanging vows hadn't stopped his father from leaving; it hadn't made his dad stick around or fight harder or love his mother enough to stay. Ryson had stopped believing in the sanctity of marriage and what it was supposed to mean the day his dad walked out.

And no matter how many times we talked about it, I couldn't get him to change his mind. As a matter of fact, he usually spent the entire discussion trying to change mine. But I refused. I believed in marriage, and more than that, I *wanted* it. I wanted to be Ryson's wife, and I wanted him to be my husband in every way possible—spiritually, soulfully, legally. If there was one single issue standing in the way of our blissfully happy future, it was that.

What is the compromise in a situation like this? I often

asked myself.

Ryson released a breath, his face pained. "I know, babe. We can talk about that later." He smirked at me, but it was only to placate me, to get me to stop talking about it.

This wasn't a conversation to have in front of all our friends even though the girls already knew the details. They'd both told me that Ryson would eventually change his mind, and I used to believe that. I wasn't so sure anymore.

I swallowed hard but stayed quiet, and Ryson took it as his cue. "Look, I think if we all did the show together, it could be brilliant. Fucking brilliant."

This part was news to me—the idea of including all of our friends—but it was perfect, and I felt myself light up from the inside out. I'd been on board with the idea of the show before, but now, I wanted to help spearhead it and make sure it got the green light, regardless of how hard we had to push to make it happen.

"I don't hate it, but how would this be different from all the other shows out there?" Paige cocked her head to the side in consideration and waited for his response.

Ryson rolled up his shirtsleeves, and I watched as the man I loved transformed into a smart and savvy businessman who worked the room, casting everyone in it under his spell. "Paige, you're the perfect example. You just had all that crap happen to you, all those lies and everything you went through in the media. I mean, what if you could control how people saw you? You're going to college now, like a normal girl. It would be amazing for people our age to see you doing the things that they're doing. Studying, writing a paper, failing a test." He laughed before taking another sip of the amber liquid. "I mean, that's what you've always wanted, right? To be relatable? This is a great way to show just how relatable you really are. Plus, this still keeps you in the public eye in a positive way while you're taking a break from acting."

I watched as Paige sucked her bottom lip into her mouth and bit on it. Her eyes crinkled together, and I knew Ryson's words were replaying inside her head.

"And, Tatum, you're the perfect example of a fish out of water."

"I'm the perfect fish out of what?" He practically choked on his own drink.

Tatum seemed content to stay in the background, but that was a difficult thing to achieve when you were dating America's sweetheart, college student or not.

"You're the guy who isn't from here, but you still got a job in the business. Anyone who wants to move to LA and pursue their dream in the entertainment industry would relate to you. You're the outsider, so the way you think, the things you do, they're different 'cause you're not from here. Plus, it would be a great way to show the public that you got your job because of your talent and hard work, not because of your girlfriend. No offense." He nudged his head toward Paige.

"None taken," Paige and Tatum said in unison, but Tatum didn't look entirely convinced.

"What, man? I thought you'd love this," Ryson said, looking almost wounded.

"It's just that I really got lucky when it came to getting my job." Tatum shrugged, and I knew he had no idea just how talented he truly was. It was an artist's curse—to constantly question if you had the tools to last or if you had simply hit a streak of good timing and luck.

"But you've kept your job because you have talent," Walker chimed in, and we all nodded and murmured our agreement. "I wouldn't keep using you if I didn't like what you produced. I don't care who you're dating."

"Thanks," Tatum said softly, clearly embarrassed by the influx of compliments.

"And, Walker, buddy," Ryson started to say, "the world in general just gives a shit about whatever it is you're doing. Always has. But with you making the transition from music to movies, it's a good angle. We can show how hard it is. You're taking acting classes, right? It's not like things are being handed to you just because of who you are. You have to actually work to secure roles, right?"

"Absolutely," Walker said.

"It's a positive message. See, guys, here's the thing. Our society is so fucked up; you know this already. That family who's on TV right now, they're everything that's wrong with our world. They project all the wrong things. I'm sure they do some admirable things behind the scenes, but they never talk about it. They never promote it. All they do is amplify how to be superficial, vain, and fake."

"Yeah, but they're bajillionaires," I added with a sick laugh.

"Because that's what they wanted to be. We already have money. And none of us are trying to sell our crappy clothes or makeup kits," Ryson interjected. "We're already successful. We're already famous."

"What are we trying to sell then? I mean, what's our angle?" I asked.

"We're not selling anything, babe. It would be more about putting the *real* back into reality TV. Show our business and our industry in a different light. Remember back when reality TV first started, and it wasn't scripted? I want to go back to that." He started talking quickly, and I knew he was getting even more amped up. "Showing what's real and what's true, without all the melodrama for the sake of ratings. We don't have to do that kind of stuff to get society to watch. They're interested in our lives and not because of any forced or fake drama. They just want to be let in."

"You're not wrong," Madison interjected, and I knew her agent wheels were spinning. "People would watch the show just because you're in it. And it's something they already want."

"I think we can make some positive changes, show the things that no one ever sees or talks about. Madison, the way you care about your clients and focus on what's in their best interests as opposed to making a buck, it's an entirely different way of thinking in Hollywood. You're the furthest thing from greedy. But that's all that so many people in this business are. I think you could inspire a whole new generation who would want to be agents for all the right reasons. They'd want to emulate you."

"Thank you, Ryson," Madison said as her cheeks turned pink. "But I don't think people want to see me on their TVs each week."

"That's where you're wrong. Not only because you're Walker's girlfriend, but the way you conduct your business is also important. It's a vital aspect to show. It *needs* to be shown. Kids need to know that it's okay to have morals and values and that you don't have to sacrifice them to be good at your job or get ahead. Plus, the fact that you and Walker have known each other since you were fifteen," he said before pausing. "Well, you know everyone will eat that right up."

Tatum sounded like he was choking on something, "Wait, what? You guys have known each other since you were fifteen?"

Madison looked flustered as she looked at Tatum. "We had a little romance one summer when we were kids."

"Little?" Walker guffawed, his face twisted in mock horror.

"Whatever. We had a summer romance, but then we never saw each other again." Madison tried to make it sound better but still failed.

I stared at Tatum's face, watching his expression grow even more confused as his eyes pulled together.

"Wait. So, how did y'all meet again? Or what happened?"

"Do you really not know this story?" I asked.

The idea that he hadn't heard about Madison and Walker was almost unbelievable to me, especially since he was Paige's live-in boyfriend.

How has she never filled him in? I wondered.

"I didn't really care about any of you people until this one crashed in my town." He thumbed toward Paige, and she looked at him, her face filled with a loving smile.

It warmed my heart to see her so happy, especially after everything she'd gone through with that dipshit ex-boyfriend of hers. He'd tried to make her the laughingstock of our industry, selling lies to whoever paid the most and embarrassing her in front of the whole damn world. No one deserved to be treated like that, particularly Paige. She was a kind person who should have been loved by the same sort of man. She had definitely found it in Tatum, and I couldn't have been happier for them.

"Fair enough," I relented, remembering that there was a whole world outside of California that didn't revolve around our antics and our business.

Walker hit his fist on the table to regain Tatum's attention. "Can you believe she didn't even recognize me, man? I pulled her onstage during one of my concerts, and she still had no idea who I was."

The silverware clanged as Tatum dropped his fork against his plate, his head shaking vigorously. "Wait, how many other Walkers are there in the world? Did you forget his name too?"

"My middle name is Walker. She didn't know me by that name," Walker tried to explain.

Tatum's expression shifted, and his head nodded in understanding.

Madison jumped in. "This is so not fair, by the way. You pulled me onstage in front of thousands of screaming fans. I was nervous, and you were hot as hell. You're lucky I didn't puke on your shoes," she finished before taking a sip of her wine.

Walker reached out to touch her hair, running his fingers through it as they smiled at one another. "So, yeah, she didn't recognize me. Had no clue. I had to pretty much harass the living shit out of her to get her to see me again," he continued around our laughter because it was true.

"Understatement of the year. Stalker." Madison rolled her eyes.

"Well, you eventually figured it out then. That you'd met each other before?" Tatum was invested in the story now, practically clamoring for more.

"Like I said, I always knew it was her. I had to remind her who I was. Then, it all fell into place." Walker reached for Madison's hand and planted a sweet kiss on top of it.

"That's a cool story though. Why aren't you writing a script and getting it produced?" Tatum asked as he finished off his drink.

"Oh my gosh. You've gone all Hollywood on us, Tatum Montgomery. What would your mother think?" Paige asked in mock horror with a thick Southern accent.

"He's right. It's a great love story," Ryson said.

"Ryson, babe?" I interrupted.

"My love," he said with a smile.

"What about us? I mean, what would we add to the show?" I wasn't trying to be stupid or naive with my question. Everyone seemed like they'd be contributing aspects that were so important and relevant to society that I simply wasn't sure what we'd add.

"We're the *it* couple," he said as if it were the most absolute thing in the world. "No offense, guys." His eyes roamed the table. "But we're the couple that everyone wants to live with on a daily basis because we've been together the longest. We would show how hard we work at balancing our relationship and our careers. Most people have no idea all the things we want to do, how many irons we have in the fire, or what it takes to be successful on and off the screen. We could show people how strong our relationship is and how nothing works if we don't. We're a team, and I think that's an important thing for people to see. In a world where career and money comes first, you and I put each other first. That's the way we work, but a lot of people don't see that as a way to be successful. They truly believe that it's one or the other."

"They're wrong," I said defensively without thinking.

"I know."

Ryson and I were a formidable team, a partnership. There was nothing and no one that got between us. We were as solid as they came, built on a strong foundation that only got stronger with time. I knew that, every day, people looked up to us and wanted the kind of love we had. They had been following our love story since the second it started. If I wasn't me, I would probably be stalking our story too.

"Come here. I want to show you something." Ryson pushed back from the table, walked to my end, and reached for my hand.

I glanced around, but no one else moved from their seats, and we weaved around them before heading toward his office down the hall.

He sat down, turned his chair in one quick swivel, and

wrapped his arms around my waist, pulling me on top of his lap. "You look so pretty tonight." His gaze swept across my face before landing on my mouth.

"So do you," I said with a slight smile because my man was anything but pretty. Sexy, rugged, charming, hot as hell? Yes. Pretty? No.

"Do I? I wore this outfit just for you," he teased.

I pressed my lips against his. Ryson's mouth opened, welcoming me in, as my brain spun the way it tended to do whenever he kissed me. His fingers fisted in the back of my hair as he slowly tugged our mouths apart, the loss immediate as cold air replaced where his lips once had been.

"Are you ready for this?" He tilted his head as his dark eyes waited for my reaction.

"Just show me already," I pleaded, not having any idea what he was about to pull up.

"Look." He pointed at the computer screen where it read *We Want a Quinn & Ryson Reality Show!* followed by 5.2 million signatures.

"Holy shit. Five-point-two million people have signed that?" I stared at the computer screen, dumbfounded.

Of course, I knew that Ryson and I were popular, and people either loved us or hated us, but I'd had no idea that *that* many people would care enough about us to sign a petition to get us on television.

"That's weird, right? I mean, that's a lot of people."

"It sure seems like a lot. Madison sent me the link and told me that if you and I had never thought about reality TV before, we should at least consider it now. Of course, I told her I'd already been kicking the idea around for months."

"Madison sent it?" I fidgeted on his lap and craned my neck to look at him. "How'd she even find that?"

"I'm not sure, but you know she's always looking out for us," he added with a smile.

"You're really serious about this. And including everyone else too?"

"Absolutely. But it would have to be done right." His tone turned stern, and I knew he'd been thinking about this for longer than even I realized.

"How so? I'm not opposed to anything you think might help our careers in a positive way, but I want to hear exactly what you're thinking."

"I'm thinking that most reality shows go one way or the other. You either end up loving the people on it even more or you hate them and wish they'd die, so you'd never have to hear about them again."

My body shuddered with his words, as I knew how true they were.

He continued, "I definitely don't want either of us to be hated, so we would have to have some kind of control over the editing process before it airs."

He stopped talking and waited for me to agree.

I encouraged him to continue, and he did, "Personally, I don't want it to be fake. All the shit that's on TV right now is such a joke. It's all scripted and filled with storylines that are beyond made up, but people think they're true. They believe everything they see, Quinn. How do they not see how fake it is?"

He was so passionate; I couldn't help but smile as I listened to him.

"I wouldn't want anything about us or our relationship to be scripted. I want people to see the truth between us, the real reality. But that means, we'll have to find a crew who has the same vision. And that might be a struggle."

I bent down and planted a kiss square on his mouth. "I wholeheartedly agree. You make me so proud, babe."

He quirked his head, and a smile stretched across his handsome face. "Why's that?"

"It's the way you think. The industrious part of your brain and the creative parts of your mind." I tapped my fingers along the top of his head. "I'm in love with them both."

"But you love what's in my pants the most, right?" he teased, grabbing my hand and firmly placing it on the hardening part beneath his jeans.

"Oh, I definitely love that but not the most." I smiled, stroking it a couple of times before leaning close to Ryson's mouth. "We have guests," I reminded my boyfriend as I moved from his lap.

"They'll be fine," he groaned. "Won't even miss us."

"After they leave, I'm all yours. Come on." I tried to pull him up by the hand, but he pulled me back down instead.

"I love you, you know," he whispered against my neck, his lips pressing against my pulse there.

"I do know. I love you too."

"I don't do anything without you, Quinn. So, if you're not on board with this, if even a percent of you isn't comfortable, we won't do it."

"I know that too," I said as my chest filled with even more love than I'd thought was possible.

I'd never known that this kind of love could actually be real, but here I was, living a damn fairy tale every single day of my life all because of the man currently holding me in his arms. I knew how lucky I was as my mind drifted off to the past, when I'd first met Ryson. Oh, how far we'd both come since we were teenagers.

FIRST MEETING

THE PAST

Quinn

T o say I was worried about my latest movie role would be the understatement of the year. For once, I was playing someone my own age—a sixteen-year-old high school junior—and although it was the typical boy-meets-nerdy-girl romance, I loved the script and couldn't wait to bring my character to life on the big screen. Just like any other girl, I'd always been drawn to Cinderella-type stories, no matter how many had been made before.

My lead costar, however, was Ryson Miller. We hadn't met yet, and I found myself a little nervous about it.

While he was nice to look at, Ryson's off-screen antics as of late were another thing altogether. Rumor had it that he had recently acquired a drug problem, which wasn't unheard of in this industry, but I always did my best to keep that kind of lifestyle far away from me.

Drugs had never appealed to me. Maybe it was because my parents were both schoolteachers, or maybe I simply didn't have the *let's get high and get fucked up* gene in my body. More than likely, it was because of an upsetting experience that had happened when I first started acting.

When I was ten years old, my director had tried to get me to do cocaine with him in his trailer. I stared at the powdery white substance, a jagged line of it spread across a small mirror, and was absolutely terrified. I had to glance down at myself to be sure I hadn't peed my pants because I was convinced at the time that I had.

The director confidently told me, "Everyone does it," and said it would help me "stay up late" at night and get through my scenes with "lots of extra energy."

At his words, my eyes instantly filled with tears. *I might only be ten*, I remembered thinking, *but I'm not stupid.*

Thank God an inner strength came bubbling up from somewhere, giving me the courage to tell him to go to hell as I walked out of his trailer. Telling a grown-up to go to hell was something I'd never thought I'd have the balls to do, especially as a ten-year-old, but by the grace of God, I had grown a well-needed pair that day.

I never told my parents what had happened, although I should have. I was terrified that they would make me stop acting or that they would tell me it was somehow my fault. Thankfully, the director cut off all nonessential communication with me and never offered me drugs again. Looking back now, I realized he had probably been afraid that I would rat him out at any moment, so he'd wisely kept his distance from me.

After that had happened, I'd made sure I was never alone

for the remainder of the shoot, always asking a costar or the on-set teacher to accompany me anywhere I had to be. Sometimes, I wondered where that conviction had come from, that lion-like inner power, and I prayed I'd always have the strength to walk away when I needed to.

Sitting in my designated chair on the set, watching all the activity going on around me, I cleared my mind of old memories, so I could focus on Ryson and his problem. Part of me wished that the studios would require all talent to stay clean during the duration of the shoot, but the thought of Hollywood trying to enforce that made me almost laugh out loud. If they insisted the talent remain drug-free, there'd be no one to star in any movies or TV shows. As sad as that was, it was the truth.

I dreaded being alone with Ryson and definitely didn't want to feel uncomfortable around him after I inevitably turned down whatever he might offer. Drugs made actors moody. Well, moodier than usual. And they messed with a person's creative ability, although some would argue that it made them even more creative, but that was a line of bullshit. I'd seen firsthand how destructive drugs could be.

As my mind played out potential scenarios that hadn't even happened yet, Ryson Miller entered through one of the stage doors and lit up the whole damn room. Everyone stopped what they were doing and turned to watch him confidently stride across the concrete floor.

My stomach flip-flopped, and I couldn't tear my eyes away from his lean frame even if I wanted to. Only eighteen, and he already had this much charisma? That didn't bode well for me.

Ryson's mussed brown hair fell into his eyes, making him seem less like a celebrity and more approachable. When he caught sight of me, a smile broke out across his face. Before I even realized it, I was smiling back at him like a love-struck groupie instead of giving him my usual professional smile.

He plopped down in the chair next to mine that had his name stenciled on the back of it and stuck out his hand. "I'm Ryson," he said as if I hadn't already known his name.

When his big hand wrapped around mind, warmth immediately flowed through my body at his touch. Ryson was so much hotter in person than I'd expected him to be, and I found myself a little rattled by his presence.

As he squeezed my hand, my gaze fell to his lips, which were incredibly kissable. Thank God we had multiple kissing scenes in this film, so I could get well acquainted with them.

"Quinn," I said softly, hoping my voice didn't sound as dreamy as I felt.

Ryson studied me for a second before he let out a long breath. "God, you're even prettier in person." Holding my gaze, he leaned forward to kiss the top of my hand.

The beginnings of a blush crept over my cheeks, but then I froze as I noticed his brown eyes were glassy, so dark that they were nearly black because his pupils were dilated. He was fucked up—on what, I wasn't sure, but he was definitely on something.

Leaning toward him, I whispered, "Are you on something?" I kept my voice quiet, not wanting to get him in trouble or to mess up our shooting schedule.

He smirked, briefly lifting his eyebrows. "You want? We can take a hit in my trailer."

Intense disappointment swept over me. I hadn't realized until now how much I wanted the rumors to be wrong. I wanted to hate Ryson for his weakness, to make my body stop responding to him the way that it was, but apparently, I was no longer in control of those things.

Dropping his hand, I said, "I don't do that stuff."

He cocked his head to the side. "What stuff exactly?"

"Any of it." I frowned and shook my head. "I don't do any of it."

"Never?"

I leaned away from him and sat up straighter. "Never."

"Not even once?"

Was my reaction really so hard to believe? "No."

"You're a good girl then, eh? I could use a good girl in my life."

Discouraged, I looked away as I said flatly, "Well, good luck finding one."

"I thought I just did."

I turned back toward him, my face dead serious as I pointed at him. "Let's make one thing perfectly clear. I would never date someone like you, Ryson Miller. It's a shame that all the stuff they say about you and drugs is true. I really wish it weren't."

He sucked in a breath and swallowed hard, his expression as hurt as if I'd physically slapped him. "Well, what if it wasn't? What if I stopped?"

"Then, maybe I'd consider it." I shrugged. "But if it's so easy to stop, then why haven't you?"

The smirk reappeared as he said, "I've never had a reason to before."

"Seriously? I'm sure that charm works on every other girl in this industry, but I'm not every other girl," I huffed, crossing my arms over my chest as I looked away, willing myself to be irritated instead of sweet on him.

Ryson paused before he laughed, a happy, carefree sound that filled the air, my ears, my heart.

"You're definitely not like every other girl. But, seriously, Quinn, I've never wanted to stop. Maybe you'll help me see the error of my ways, make me a better person and all that jazz."

He sounded so sincere that I glanced back at him. When I did, he winked, and for some reason, it pissed me off.

"You should really want all that for yourself," I spat back in a low voice. "You shouldn't need a reason to quit other than you want to stop being an idiot and ruining your life."

I shook my head, furious that Ryson was so self-indulgent. Hopefully, he wouldn't be a total waste during our shoot. His actions could completely ruin this movie for us, and I'd be damned if I let him do that.

"You're making this difficult," he said with a groan.

"Well, I'm not a miracle worker."

"I think you might be."

A production assistant shuffled past us as she crossed the stage, her black ponytail bobbing from side to side as she mumbled something into the microphone attached to her headpiece. Catching Ryson's eye as she passed, she lifted her chin and said, "Ryson, you're needed in makeup."

Ryson pushed himself out of his chair and stood in front of me, settling his body between my legs and leaning in close enough that I could smell his spearmint gum.

"If I feel about you at the end of this movie the way I feel about you right now, I'll never touch another drug for the rest of my life. And you, Quinn Johnson, will be my girl for all of it."

My cheeks burned as I tilted my head back to meet his gaze. Something in my chest tightened, making it hard for me to breathe. No guy had ever been so direct with me before, so demanding and bossy, and I hated how much I liked it.

An uncomfortable laugh sputtered from me. "Are you always this cocky?"

"Only when I see something I want," he said, his tone serious. "Better watch out."

With those words, Ryson walked away and left me staring after him with my mouth hanging open.

What the hell have I just gotten myself into?

LIFE CHANGES
THE PRESENT
Quinn

ALL OF OUR friends left with a renewed sense of excitement after Ryson's announcement during dinner. It was fun to think about doing a show with those closest to me, but it was also a little scary.

I checked my email one last time and noticed an urgent one from our agent, marked with a red exclamation point.

"Ryson," I said.

He stopped moving as I read the email out loud, pulling out a barstool and sitting.

"I can't believe Sammy's retiring." I glanced across the kitchen table at Ryson's face.

He shrugged with my words before giving me a half-frown. Sammy had been our agent for our entire careers. Neither one of us knew this career without him.

"He is, like, a hundred, Quinn. We both knew this day would come eventually."

Ryson was right, but it did nothing to stop the butterflies

from flapping nervously in my stomach. Part of me hated change, even when it was something I knew might be for the best. I'd been talking about getting a new agent for years, before I'd even met Madison. I wanted someone younger with a more evolved way of thinking since the times had changed and Sammy seemed hesitant to adapt.

Part of me wanted to take more risks, but Sammy always talked me out of it, and I obediently went along with his guidance, too skittish to go against him. I thought the scariest part about change was all of the unknown. What if I tried something new and it failed or was a total flop?

"The agency wants to meet with us, so we can decide on a new agent within the company." I exhaled, and my lungs deflated like a limp balloon. I felt trapped somehow even though I wasn't.

"Maybe we should jump ship completely." Ryson tilted his head at me and raised his brows. "I mean, if we have to choose a new agent anyway, what's the difference between staying with them or going somewhere new? A brand-new person is a brand-new person, no matter what agency they're with." He wasn't wrong. "And you and I both know that Madison would be a better fit for us. I think we should set up a meeting with her before we meet with Sammy and the team. That way, we can have some more perspective before we hear their presentation. I don't want to feel pressured or obligated to stay with them."

"I don't either." As soon as the words left my mouth, the realization hit. I had felt guilty for thinking about leaving a place that had done me right by me for so many years. But I knew it was time for a change, and I didn't want to feel suckered into staying. "I want to work with Madison," I said, and a weight instantly lifted itself from my shoulders.

Ryson smiled. "I know you do."

I smiled back, feeling light. "I'm going to call her right now."

"Now?" He glanced at his all-black watch. A watch I had given him last year for our anniversary. "She just left."

"She won't care." I laughed back at him and smiled. "And I'm too excited to wait."

But my enthusiasm would have to be delayed because the little wench sent me straight to voice mail.

★ ★ ★

MADISON FINALLY CALLED me back the next morning, and I wandered into the backyard to take the call. Feeling the sun on my body, I sat on one of the loungers and stretched, filling Madison in.

The first words out of her mouth were, "That sucks about Sammy," quickly followed by, "But it's about time."

We discussed the details about us leaving the company and joining hers. Neither one of us needed much convincing, but I had to make sure that she had the capacity to take us on. The last thing I wanted to do was put her in a position she wasn't able to handle with a client list that was too big for one person. Madison convinced me that she was more than capable of handling the roster of clients she currently had and that she'd secretly always held out space for two more, hoping that we'd sign with her at some point.

I hung up, and elation coursed through every inch of me. My career had always given me a thrill, but this was something more. This felt like the start of something new and fresh. A brand-new world was about to open to me and Ryson, and it felt amazing. I felt like we could do anything we put our minds to and that we'd finally have the support behind us that neither one of us had known we were missing. A new era was about to begin; I sensed it.

"Ryson!" I shouted from the backyard, hoping he could hear me from wherever he was in the house.

"Yeah?" His head poked out from the kitchen, and I waved him over.

I moved from the chair and toward the edge of our pool, dipping my toes in the water.

Ryson sat next to me and rested his hand on my thigh. "So," he slowly dragged out, "what'd she say?"

"She can't wait for us to finally sign with her. Said she's glad she didn't hold her breath, waiting, or she would be dead by now," I said with a smile, and Ryson laughed, his whole body shaking with the gesture. "And ... are you ready?"

His brows shot up as he sucked in a loud breath before asking, "Ready for what?"

"She talked to Howard freaking Sampson about the reality show."

Ryson's jaw dropped as his face lit up. "Seriously? She talked to Howard? Why? About what?"

Ryson rarely got starstruck, but he'd respected and idolized Howard for years on a professional level. It was the cutest thing I'd ever seen, watching him get like this.

"Well, you know that's her old roommate's dad, right? Her good friend Keri?"

Ryson's expression morphed into understanding. "That's right. But Howard's a big-budget blockbuster movie producer. Why would he give a shit about a little low-budget reality show?"

My lips turned upward. "Because, apparently, Madison had a short list of people she thought wouldn't turn the show into something we didn't want it to be. She knew we wanted to keep it realistic and how adamant we all were about it not being scripted or fake. So, she took her list to Howard to get his professional opinion, and he freaking said ..." I paused for effect.

Ryson reached for my shoulders and shook them. "He said what, Quinn? What did he say?"

Ryson was coming unglued, and it was such rare form for him to be in that I almost didn't want to give in and tell him.

"Quinn!" he shouted once more.

I started laughing. "Okay, okay. Sorry. You're just so cute right now. He said that he wants to do it."

Ryson paled, his hands dropping from my body. "He said he wants to do what?"

"The show. Our show. Howard Sampson wants to produce our show. With one caveat." I grinned again and could tell that I was pushing Ryson a little too far.

"Quinn, put me out of my misery and just tell me, please. Stop with the games. My heart can't take it."

"He wants you to direct it."

Ryson jumped up from the ground and into the air. "Are you kidding me?" He spun around and yelled before reaching for me and pulling me straight to my feet. "Are you joking?" His strong arms tugged me against his body, and he kissed me hard. "This is real?"

"It's real," I answered with tears in my eyes because seeing Ryson this happy filled me with joy. "I guess Madison had been feeling him out for a little while now. She used to live with his daughter, remember? She got him to confirm his interest right after she left our house."

I didn't spare Ryson a single detail on how Madison's mind worked and how quickly she had made things happen. It was exactly why everyone wanted to be repped by her. She went above and beyond for her clients, and she fought for them when no one else would.

"I can't believe this is happening. I can't believe Howard even wants to be involved in a project like this. Did he say why?" Ryson questioned, and I couldn't blame him.

I had asked Madison the same exact thing. It didn't make any sense really—why a man like him would want to do something like this.

"He said that he wanted to try something new. And he liked the way Madison had pitched the idea for the show," I said before adding, "He might have mentioned something about absolutely hating the state of reality TV these days and that being a part of a movement to change it was something that he thought was important and necessary. He said he feared for our youth and was happy he'd be dead by the time they took over."

Ryson laughed. "Can't argue with any of that. I think we all feel the same way."

"We definitely do."

"Okay then, so the show is on. And signing with Madison is on. Am I missing anything?"

"Nope. You're all caught up."

"Then, it's time I take my woman inside and show her how grateful I am that she's mine." His eyes narrowed as his tongue darted out and licked his bottom lip. "Unless you want me to take you right here," he said, taking two steps toward me.

Instead of running away, I stood firm. "Choice is yours, Mr. Director," I said and waited to see how he'd react.

His face broke out into a devilish grin as he closed the space between us and scooped me into his arms. He carried me into our bedroom and gently placed me down on top of our bed where he made love to me in the most tender way, leaving no part of my skin untouched. I wasn't always sure which Ryson I would get in the bedroom, but I loved each and every version of him.

My head pressed against Ryson's chest as his fingers ran through my hair. We were the kind of couple who cuddled after sex. After connecting in such an intimate way, it never felt right to get up, get dressed, and carry on like nothing had just happened. We both liked to stay in the afterglow a bit longer, our sweaty bodies still touching as our heart rates slowed.

"Do you have any concerns? With the show, I mean?"

My chest tightened a little in response to his question, and I wondered how on earth he could tell that I had the smallest issue blooming to life inside of me. Pulling my head up, I propped myself on my elbows and looked into his eyes. "A little," I said, hesitating.

Ryson sat up, stacking the pillows behind him. "Tell me."

"Promise you won't get mad?" I said, and his body tensed.

No good conversation started with that sentence. And while Ryson and I didn't fight often, we still had disagreements and arguments from time to time. We were two passionate, strong-willed people who each had their own baggage to work through. But when you found the right person, they were the one worth unpacking it all for.

"Quinn," he said my name softly. "What is it?"

I sucked in a deep breath because I absolutely hated having this conversation. Mostly because I always felt like I was on the losing side of it. "I'm worried about the whole marriage thing."

"What whole marriage thing?" he asked as a crease formed between his eyes.

"That I want to get engaged and married, and you don't."

Saying it out loud to Ryson always seemed to hurt a little more than talking about it with my girlfriends. It was probably because Ryson had the power to change the outcome of our situation, and I knew he didn't want to.

"You're worried about it coming up on the show?" he asked as though it'd never crossed his mind. And to be fair, it probably hadn't.

But it had been the one thing on my mind since we first started talking about it a few months back. The idea that everyone would see us together and that they'd know we weren't ever going to get engaged because my boyfriend didn't want to marry me was unsettling.

I nodded. "I'm worried about it coming up on the show, yes," I repeated.

Ryson placed the back of his hand on my cheek, and my eyes closed instinctively with his touch.

"I might not believe in marriage, Quinn, but I believe in us."

"I know." I let out a small breath.

We'd had this conversation a thousand times before. I'd heard it all. He'd heard it all. We'd talked it to death. But for some reason, I couldn't let it go. I probably never would. At least, not until there was a ring on my finger.

"A piece of paper doesn't change anything between us. A ring on your finger doesn't either," he added, as if reading my mind.

This point of view of his wasn't new news to me. Blah, blah, blah. I hated this particular argument.

I wanted to take the next step in our relationship. I was ready for it. And I wasn't saying that we needed to get married tomorrow, but I did eventually want to be married. It wasn't about the piece of paper to me. It was more than that. And the fact that Ryson didn't share the same feelings on this subject matter hurt.

"I know that's all you think a marriage is ... a piece of paper. But it's more than that to me. You're the person I want to be with for the rest of my life. And I know you feel the same way about me. Why do you push back on this so hard?"

"I don't want to be with anyone else on this planet. Ever. I hope you know that," he said, and I nodded because I did know that. I never questioned Ryson's love for me. "We don't have to be married to know how much we mean to each other, right? Do you think I'm going to love you more after I say some vows? They have nothing to do with how I feel about you."

"I mean, I guess you're right," I said delicately, relenting even though I sort of hated myself for giving in when it wasn't how I truly felt. "It's just," I stumbled before finding my words, "I think that marriage is about making a commitment. Making a promise to each other and saying vows that stand for something."

"Saying some words doesn't keep you faithful. Vows don't keep couples together. They're just words, Quinn. A script, if you think about it. Words that people say all the time, every single day, and then ten years down the road, they don't mean them anymore. Things change. People change. And the vows, the promises, the piece of paper, the labels"—his voice started to rise, and I knew he was getting riled up—"they don't mean shit. They contribute to nothing. Maybe if people weren't married, they wouldn't take each other for granted. Maybe being married makes couples lazy. They feel like they don't have to work so hard to keep the other person anymore."

This was how our conversations about this topic always ended up going. Ryson took it personally. His parents' failed marriage, the fact that his dad had walked away and never come back—it soured him to the whole concept. It made him stop believing that marriage was a natural step in the evolution of a couple or that it could even be a good thing. He couldn't seem to separate himself from what had happened to his parents. In his mind, it was all connected. And how could I argue against that, against the reality of how he felt in his heart?

"I want to be your wife. And I want you to be my husband. I want to say those words. They mean something to me."

"Then, call me your husband. I'll call you my wife. We can make vows to each other right here in this bed. It's all the same to me."

"It's not the same to me," I said quietly even though Ryson had already known all of this.

My eyes started to water because I knew I was losing this fight … *again.*

"Quinn," he said my name, willing me to look at him. "Baby, please. Please look at me," he begged, and I did as he'd asked. "I love you so damn much. More than anything in this world. I never want to live a single day without you. I want to spend the rest of my life with you. Just because I don't want to get married, it doesn't change anything. I would still slay every dragon for you. I always will. I just don't feel like I have to marry you to prove that," he said, his brown eyes pleading with me for understanding.

I watched as his Adam's apple bobbed as he swallowed, and I knew with all my heart that he meant every word he had just said. I also knew in my guts that if I gave Ryson an ultimatum, if I told him that it was marriage or me, he would pick me ten times out of ten. But I hated even thinking that. The last thing I wanted to do was force Ryson into something he didn't believe in. How could you do that to someone you loved and expect them not to hate you for it sooner or later?

"I'm just ready for more, is all. And you aren't. And I need to be okay with that," I said even though I wasn't. For whatever female, breeding reason, I wasn't.

He stayed quiet for a heartbeat or two before speaking, "I know this is hard because we have such different views on the subject, but I think it could be good for the show. We can't be the only couple on the planet going through this exact same thing."

It took me only a second to catch up and get back on his reality show train of thought. "I just feel like that might be crossing a line for me into territory that's a little too personal. I'm okay with opening up and allowing cameras into certain parts of my life, but I'm not sure about this particular part. This is my heart we're talking about."

"And mine."

Sucking in a long breath as thoughts danced in my head, one hit me with a force so hard that I knew I had to say it out loud. "I think I'd be embarrassed," I said the words and realized instantly how true they were. I hadn't even put it together before this moment.

Ryson moved his arms and reached for me, pulling me closer to him. "Why would you be embarrassed?" His fingers moved through the long blonde strands of my hair.

"Because my boyfriend of the last five years doesn't want to marry me. And he will tell the whole world that simple fact. And I'll feel like there's something wrong with me. Like I'm not worth marrying. Or that you don't love me enough to make me your wife."

He cut me off, "But this has nothing to do with the way I feel about you. I could not love someone more than I love you."

"But what if it is about me, and you just don't realize it? What if you met someone else and were willing to marry her?"

His head shook slowly and deliberately as a small smile ghosted across his lips. "Quinn, that would never in a million years happen. Not while I'm breathing. Do you hear me? There is no one else I want to be with for the rest of my life than you. No other woman could own my heart and soul. No one could ever know me, truly know me, the way that you do. You saved me. You know that, right?"

I nodded because I did know. I had saved him. And I'd do it all over again if I had to.

"I'll tell the world how I feel about you, Quinn. No one who watches our show will question my love or loyalty or dedication to you. And we absolutely do not have to talk about marriage if you don't want to. We call the shots. We're in control here. Just think about it before you rule it out. Think about the conversations we could inspire. The good we could do," he said in his typical Ryson way. He was always fired up to make a change and potentially do good in a society he felt was lacking. "No one talks about this kind of thing."

"I'll think about it," I promised.

I looked at the man I knew I would love until the day I died, and my heart broke at the thought of never being able to call him my husband. I had no idea why it was so important to me or why it meant so much. All I knew was that it did. My life would feel incomplete somehow if we never got to exchange vows, make promises, and share a last name.

Is that stupid? I wondered. *Is it an antiquated and out-of-date notion?*

Maybe Ryson was right; talking about this on the show would probably inspire honest conversation between couples and people in general. And maybe it would help me feel less alone.

And as excited as I was for my girls Madison and Paige to get married one day, I knew that when the day came, a part of me would be envious and jealous.

In my close-knit circle of friends, everyone always joked that Ryson and I would be the first to get married. I used to believe it too. A part of me always thought that Ryson would eventually change his mind.

As females, why do we do that? I wondered. *Never believe what a guy told us and always convince ourselves that their opinion would change with time or that we could change it?*

So, yeah, maybe talking about it would be a good thing. I just wasn't sure that I wanted to be *that* exposed and vulnerable in front of the entire world.

Did I really want to become the spokeswoman for guys

who wouldn't marry their girlfriends? Because that was exactly what I'd become.

Remember when they dubbed Kate Middleton "Waity Katie"?

I only imagined what they'd start calling me.

THE LOVE DOCTOR
Ryson

T O BE HONEST, things had been a little tense after our marriage conversation last night. Quinn and I ate breakfast together, and while I tried my best to be affectionate and sweet, I could sense that she was off, a little distant and quieter. Getting married was the one subject that always divided us straight down the middle and ended up hurting her feelings and leaving me feeling frustrated. I hated whenever the topic came up, but the truth was that it was always there, lingering, even when we weren't talking about it out loud.

The shittiest part was that there wasn't really a compromise for something like this. I'd thought it over a million times, trying to find a way that would make us both happy, but I could never figure one out. Thinking about this topic always gave me a headache. I fucking hated situations that I couldn't fix or at least find a temporary solution for.

The end result always meant that one person would be sacrificing their beliefs for the other.

I knew that sacrifice and compromise were part of a healthy relationship, but how did you carry on without any kind of resentment when you sacrificed on something that big? I knew that if it came down to it, I'd do whatever it took to make Quinn happy, but I didn't want to hate her for it twenty years down the road. That was my biggest concern and fear—that I'd give in for Quinn's heart, but deep down, I'd be angry with her for making me do it.

I wasn't sure exactly how I'd feel about it in the future. The only thing I did know for sure was that I'd hate myself if I ever lost Quinn. I needed her in my life the same way I needed air to breathe, and those feelings would never change. Not as long as I was alive. My mind replayed how it felt when I'd first laid eyes on her on set all those years ago. Remembering that day was something I did often to make sure I never took her for granted or forgot what my life might be like without her. She'd saved me. I had been a total mess and didn't deserve being saved, yet she'd still saved me.

Quinn Johnson was like a dream, every teenage boy's fantasy girl. But she was going to be my reality; I'd make sure of it.

Even though she'd made it perfectly clear that this version of me would never have a shot with her, I knew she'd only half-meant it. I could have worn her down, but I'd have hated myself for it, for ruining her or bringing her down to the hell I was currently drowning in.

I'd lied when I told her that I never wanted to stop using drugs. There was nothing I wanted more than to stop doing the shit I was doing, but I was having problems with that. It wasn't as easy as I'd figured it would be to quit once I started.

I should have never fucking started. But it was too late for that now. What was done was done and all that.

Contrary to certain tabloid reports, I hadn't been using since I was twelve. Twelve, seriously? My drug habit was something I'd more recently acquired.

My dad had ditched my mom and me, claiming he'd had enough of this crazy lifestyle and her coldness.

It's not fair, *I remembered thinking,* that he said that about her.

My mom was a psychiatrist, so she handled things differently than most people, I'd come to learn.

My dad had packed his bags and moved out the same night, and I hadn't heard from him since. Not a single fucking peep.

Expecting my mom to break down, I'd braced myself to pick up all of her broken pieces, but she never did. She never even cried—not a single tear or a solitary sniffle. I remembered how she'd sucked in a long, deep breath, taken one hard look at me, squeezed my hands, and told me that we were going to be okay. Then, she hugged me, too tight really, before walking into her bedroom and closing the door behind her.

I pressed my ear to the white paneled wood to hear if she was breaking down the way I wanted to, but I didn't hear a thing. Not a single sound. I wasn't sure what she was doing in there, but it sure as hell wasn't crying.

I'd convinced myself from that night forward that if my mom wasn't crying over my dad leaving, then I sure as shit couldn't cry about it either. So, I hadn't. I was the man of the house now.

That was a little over six months ago.

I'd started acting out on set. Typical, right? Instead of acknowledging my pain, I buried it. My mom called me out on it, telling me that I was displaying classic deflection behavior. That was her official psychiatric diagnosis. She tried to get me to talk about my feelings, but I refused, telling her that I felt nothing, so there was nothing to say. As long as she seemed okay—and she really did seem okay—I pretended to be as well ... for her sake, never even thinking about the fact that she was most likely doing the same for me.

Eventually, my buried pain manifested itself into some very righteous teenage anger. I started messing up my lines at work on purpose. I threw things during meals at craft services, complaining that they were trying to poison me or intentionally make me sick. I turned into an all-around dick. Anything to get attention. My peers noticed. The paparazzi noticed. The internet noticed. Everyone noticed, except my dad. And if he had noticed, he never reached out to let me know. It only fueled my insolence more. The attention from everyone on the planet was better than none at all even if it was all negative.

My anger completely took over my life and my attitude and didn't seem to be fading. I refused to talk to my mom or let her diagnose me or medicate me.

It was only once my slightly older costars cornered me and asked what the hell had happened to the happy-go-lucky kid they'd been working with that I spilled my guts. The three of them decided I needed some help to bring back my happy. They introduced me to cocaine. Trusting my fellow actors' words about the drugs simply being there when I needed the pick-me-up and that I could stop anytime I wanted, I tried it.

And then I tried it again.

And again.

And I never wanted to stop.

Because everything was absolutely fucking perfect when I was high. It was the best fucking feeling in the whole damn galaxy, but it never lasted. The second I started to crash, I would use again. And then I spent the rest of my time chasing the way the drugs had made me feel the first time I used them. That was an unattainable goal, but it didn't stop me from trying to reach it.

As long as I was high, I felt invincible, happy, and didn't give two shits that my dad had left our family for what seemed like no reason at all. Plus, I felt like myself again. No, scratch that. I felt like an even better version of myself. Coked-up Ryson Miller was a happier, better actor. He was a better friend, a better son, a better listener, a better human being! Everything was better as long as I was using.

My mom even noticed my new and improved attitude. I did my best to make sure she didn't catch on to what I was doing, but she made it easy by burying herself in work. She had so many new clients that our paths rarely crossed at home. Plus, I was a great liar; it was my profession after all.

When the shoot had finally ended and I'd tried to quit, I'd realized that I couldn't. Nothing felt worse than coming down from the high. I'd never felt so low, so inferior, so helpless, so sad. No one had warned me what it would be like to try to stop cold turkey. That wasn't me placing blame; I was just saying. I had been fucking clueless about this coke shit and what it would do to my senses and mental state.

So, there I was, still addicted, still hoping I'd be able to stop but not really knowing how to do exactly that. I'd tried, but it'd been a half-assed effort at best. I didn't know what I was doing, and I didn't know how to quit. I should have told my mom, but I hated the idea of disappointing her with something like this. A drug-addicted son. God, would she be disappointed and then angry with herself for not seeing the signs.

I needed professional help, but a stint in rehab wasn't really on the agenda, considering my calendar was booked solid for the next thirteen months.

I hoped I'd still be alive in thirteen months.

If I was dead, I couldn't date Quinn Johnson, and dating her was definitely on the agenda for the rest of my life.

A knock at the front door broke me out of my trance, and I was grateful for the distraction. Few people could get through the gates and make it to our actual door, so I threw it open without a second thought and found Tatum standing there, staring back at me.

"Special delivery." He handed me a stack of papers, and I pulled the door all the way open.

"What is this?" I thumbed through them, recognizing Madison's logo at the top.

"Madison asked me to drop them off," he said with a

shrug as he stepped into the house.

"It's our new management contract. But we already signed these online," I said.

"She wanted you to have hard copies, I guess."

"But we could have printed out our own."

"Bro, I just do what I'm told. We saw them for breakfast before everyone split for other meetings. She asked me to drop them off, and here I am. Aren't you happy to see me?"

He batted his lashes, and I punched him in the arm.

"You know I am."

We moved through the house and toward the kitchen.

"Hey, gorgeous," Tatum said to Quinn.

She hugged him with more affection than she'd given me this morning. I was a jealous bastard but did my best to tamp it down.

"Why are you here? Can't get enough of us?" She wagged her eyebrows, and he laughed.

My jealousy sprang back to life. I was ridiculous.

"He dropped off our contracts with Madison," I said before turning to Tatum. "Gonna stay and hang out for a bit?"

"Definitely. Take me to your pool or lose me forever," Tatum mocked, and I shot him a look as we headed outside.

We'd been sitting in the backyard for the last hour, talking about the reality show. Once it was officially approved— or green-lit in Hollywood terms—I knew that things would escalate fairly quickly, and I wanted to make sure Tatum wasn't caught off guard. I needed him to be comfortable, to know what to expect, and ask any questions he might have before we dived headfirst into filming.

Thankfully, Tatum was a pretty laid-back guy who had not only adjusted to the idea of the show, but was also actually excited about it. I knew Paige had had a hand in that, but regardless, I was thrilled at how things seemed to be falling together so easily and quickly. He had been my biggest concern, the one I worried about the most, since he was the only one of us without a celebrity background.

Paige had found him after she ran away from Hollywood. Or I guessed the truth was that Tatum had found her. Regardless, he wasn't pretentious or one of those *let's move to LA to get insta-famous* types. He was the most down-to-earth and genuine guy I knew.

"Why are you frowning?" He slapped at my shoulder from the lounge chair next to mine.

I faced him, figuring that if the whole world was about to know the single thing that stood between Quinn and her dream wedding, our closest friends should too. "Just thinking."

"About?" He rolled his hand to encourage me to fill him in.

"Quinn and I got into it last night," I said before looking over my shoulder to make sure she was still inside the house and hadn't moved outside without me hearing. I didn't want her overhearing anything I said and taking it the wrong way.

"You two got into it? About what? You guys never fight." He leaned back against his lounger, his arms behind his head as the sun beat down on us both.

"Marriage." One word. A thousand reactions.

"What about it?" Tatum sounded bored. "She wants to get married next week, and you want to get married tomorrow?" he said with a laugh.

I realized that I'd never fully filled him in on my screwed-up past. "No. I don't think I want to get married at all."

That got his attention. He shot straight up, swung his legs over the lounge chair, and faced me, pulling down his sunglasses. "What do you mean, you don't want to get married? That's stupid. You're an idiot."

"You're an idiot," I shot back, sounding like a five-year-old.

"I'm not the one who doesn't want to get married," he fired back.

"So, that makes me an idiot? Because I'm nontraditional?"

He shook his head before making fun of my word choice. "Nontraditional, my ass. I'm sure Quinn loves this."

"Hence why I just told you we got into it last night."

"Well, I'd get into it too. Of course she wants to get married. You've been together a hundred years. You're the most solid couple I know. Or at least, you were up until about thirty seconds ago."

"We're still solid. Nothing's changed!" I tried to argue, but Tatum was a Southern gentleman, so he would never see things my way.

"No." He pushed his sunglasses back in place and lay back down, dismissing my response as if it were nonsense.

"No what?"

"No. You can't *not* marry Quinn," he said like I was a total dumbass who had zero say in the matter.

"And why not?" I asked with a laugh.

"Because … don't you want to have kids?"

"Yeah. I'm not sure what you learned where you're from, but kids aren't a result of marriage. Do you know how babies are made?"

"Don't be an asshole." He sat up again. The guy refused to sit still. "Fine. Let's talk about this. Why don't you want to get married? To anyone? Or you just don't want to marry Quinn?" he said the last part with a scowl on his face, his tone bitter.

He knew exactly what he was doing—pushing my buttons and riling me up.

My stomach twisted. "If I ever got married, it would only be to her. But I don't think it's necessary. I think it's a false attribute, and I don't see the point," I said the words in a harsher tone than I'd intended, but I still meant them.

"A false attribute?" he asked through a howling laugh. "Is this a California thing?"

I cocked my head to the side and closed my eyes for a second. "It's a Ryson thing."

"I can't believe I'm about to Dr. Phil your ass, but give it to me." He waved both hands in the air. "Tell me what your hang-up is."

"My hang-up?"

"Yep. Something happened in your past to make you feel this way. What is it?"

I filled Tatum in on my parents. How I'd thought they

were solid and would always be together until the day my dad upped and left without sparing us a second glance. I'd still never heard from him after all this time, and even though I knew my father's actions were all about him, they still affected me.

"That's harsh, man. I had no idea," Tatum said, his tone turning sad. "I know what it's like to not have a father."

"I know you do. But yours didn't leave you by choice," I said.

Tatum had lost his dad in a tragic accident. He'd been the one to find the body. I involuntarily shuddered at the thought.

"Doesn't make it any easier. He's still gone," he said matter-of-factly.

"True," I agreed with a nod.

"Anyway, what does your dad leaving have to do with you and Quinn? Nothing. Not a damn thing. You're not your dad."

His words were true; I knew that much. But I'd held on to that particular bitterness for so long that it became a part of me. I wasn't sure how to separate it anymore. Or even if I could.

I must have stayed quiet for too long, not answering his question, because Tatum took my silence as a sign that I was done with the topic.

"We don't have to talk about this, but I will say just one more thing." He held up a single finger. "A smart man knows that what it took to get the girl is what it takes to keep the girl," he offered with a wistful smile. "My dad used to say that. He told me not to get complacent when it came to my relationships. He said that complacency bred resentment. And that resentment was the death of love."

"Your dad sounds like a good man," I offered, silently wishing that I could have met him and wondering what he would have thought of his son now. I knew he would have loved Paige. Everyone loved Paige.

"He was the best. Truly."

I could tell that Tatum was starting to get lost in the kind of memories that took some time to pull yourself out of, so I changed the subject slightly. "So, you're going to start making public declarations of your love for Paige a weekly thing then? You know, to go off the whole *what it took to get the girl* concept," I asked, busting his balls about the interview he'd done to win Paige back.

"Probably. If this reality show gets picked up, I am," he said through a forced smile.

I laughed. "I will tell you this. I might not believe in marriage, but I know what it's like to not have Quinn in my life. To want her but not be able to have her was the worst kind of hell for me." I stopped. "That's not to say that there aren't days I want to put a muzzle on the girl just so she'll shut up for two seconds. She drives me crazy sometimes, but I know what it's like to live without her. And my life is infinitely better with her in it."

Tatum groaned. "Dude, pretty sure you should be saying all this shit to her and not me. Plus, if you're so in love with her, then it's stupid of you to not marry her."

"My feelings for her won't change because of some vows and a piece of paper."

"I get what you're saying."

"But you don't see it the same way?" I asked him, knowing full well he didn't.

"Hell no. I can't wait to marry Paige. I'd probably ask her later tonight if I knew she wouldn't freak out about it and start worrying about the paparazzi and her school." He laughed. "I still have no idea how I got this lucky. I've got to put a ring on it before she wises up and changes her mind. And you"—he pointed a finger right at me—"are just being stubborn and stupid."

"Really?"

"Yeah. Quinn wants to get married to you, you idiot."

"That she does."

"And sometimes, we have to do the things that make our girls happy so that we're not doing the shit that makes them sad."

His words struck a chord somewhere deep inside me. I replayed them in my head, chewed on them, dissected them, and memorized them before asking, "Is there anything Paige wanted that you didn't?"

A loud sound escaped. "Ryson, look around. I live in Los Angeles. Never in a million years would I have moved here if it wasn't for her. I had no desire to be here."

"Fair point. But," I said, ready to argue, "you're happy here, right?"

"Yeah, I actually love it. But you'd be happy, too, if you married Quinn. Nothing would change, except her last name." He grinned before it dropped. "Shit, probably not even that. You Hollywood people keep your last names, don't you?"

I knew he was suddenly thinking about his own situation and not mine. "Do you want Paige to change her last name?"

"Personally, yes. Professionally for her, I know it probably doesn't make sense."

"She can do that. She can legally change it but still go by Paige Lockwood for acting."

"I'd never thought about it before. I just always assumed, you know? There's still so much I don't know about this business." He sounded a little dejected, and I felt bad about it because I knew it was my fault for bringing the subject up. "Anyway, back to you and Q. Nothing would change between you guys if you said a few vows and signed a few papers."

"Maybe you're right." I blew out a small breath, considering his point more than I ever had with Quinn, and that alone made me feel like a dick.

"I am a thousand percent right," he said before pushing up from his lounger and rising to his feet, glancing at his watch.

"I'll think about it more once we're in the water. Let's go surfing."

I'd taught Tatum how to surf, and I knew he loved it as much as I did. There was something about being in the water that centered you like nowhere else could. It'd started as a replacement for the drugs but turned into my solitude.

"I wish I could, but I've got to meet my future bride." He reached for my hand and gave it a firm shake. "You'd be a fool to lose Quinn over something like this. Ask yourself why you're digging your heels in so hard. You're being stubborn and forcing your point, but why?"

It was a fair question. *Why was I so unwilling to compromise on this? What the hell was I trying to prove anyway?*

Walking Tatum outside, I gave him a wave as he hopped into his truck and pulled out of the drive. I walked back inside the house and found Quinn sipping lemonade at the kitchen counter, watching my every move with her gorgeous hazel eyes.

"Do you care if I go surf for a while?"

Her expression looked dejected for only a second before she recovered. My girl was an actress after all, and I should have seen through it, but I wanted to get in the water so badly that I gave her feelings less weight than my own.

"Nope. Go. Have fun. I'll just see you later, I guess."

She was disappointed, and I knew it, but I grabbed my board anyway.

"I love you," I said, pressing a kiss to her forehead.

"I love you." I knew she meant it even though her tone sounded like the opposite.

Everything about us was off, and I hated it but felt like I couldn't fix it. It was so unnatural for things to be this way between us, and it affected everything. I should have stayed by her side, but I was so desperate to get away and think. Tatum had asked me some questions that I wanted to delve more into, and I convinced myself that the only way to do that was to be alone.

That was my first mistake.

The second was actually leaving the house.

I should have made an effort to be with Quinn and talk it out. I should have stayed. I couldn't have known the consequences that actually leaving would have on my life. If I had, I wouldn't have left this kitchen without her. Hell, I wouldn't have left her at all.

ANNOYED AND EXHAUSTED
Quinn

L AST NIGHT'S ARGUMENT, or whatever you'd call it, still lingered. I'd wanted to feel better this morning when I woke up, but all I did was continue hearing Ryson's words in my head. Considering myself a fairly reasonable woman, I tried to figure out why this particular issue meant so much to me. *Would being married really change anything between us?* I knew that, realistically, it wouldn't, but I still wanted it, for no reason other than it was what my heart desired. It was a decision based on emotion, not logic.

Once Tatum had left, I'd thought Ryson would want to spend time together. He had to feel this unease between us the same way I did. But instead of staying, he had gone surfing. Normally, I'd be more understanding, but for whatever reason, I was pissed and hurt. We were usually so connected and in tune with each other, but he left me alone with my thoughts, and I was already exhausted from overthinking them.

Reaching for my phone, I called Paige.

"Hey," she said, sounding cheerful and happy.

"What are you doing right now?"

"Meeting Tatum. Why? Are you okay?" Her tone turned to concern, but I blew her off.

"Oh, I'm fine. Ryson just left to go surfing, so I wanted to hang out, but I'm good." Lies, lies, lies. It was funny how none of us saw through our ability to act so well.

"You sure?"

"Yeah. Call me later," I said before hanging up and wondering what to do with myself.

Walking into the office, I pulled the pile of unread scripts I had sitting on my desk and started to finger through them, seeing if any grabbed my attention.

Before I knew it, over an hour had flown by. I'd always found it interesting what a good script could do to a reader. With the power that words held, they could make you lose track of time, drag you from your internal thoughts, and completely immerse you in another world. When you felt that connected to a character on a page, you knew it was good writing. Smiling to myself, I scribbled some notes in the margin of the script as my cell phone chirped with an alert.

Finishing up my notes, I reached for my phone, assuming it would be a text message from Ryson. Most likely, he would apologize for having left, tell me that he missed me, and then ask if I wanted him to bring home any food.

I pressed my thumb to my screen, and it lit up, the unread text message blaring to life. It wasn't from Ryson, but his name was in the message. I had set up a text alerting system for both myself and Ryson's names with specific keywords. This was one of only a handful of times that a message had come through on my phone.

TEXT ALERT: Ryson Miller reportedly in accident. Status unknown.

Wait, what?

In that moment, everything inside me disconnected. My brain could no longer make sense of what I was reading. My eyes stumbled over the words as I willed the message to change or rearrange itself somehow. My lungs felt like they had caved in on me as I struggled to take in air, and my legs shook. My heart sputtered, and I was half-convinced that it would stop beating altogether. I pulled up Ryson's Contact info and pressed Send, hoping beyond all hope that this message was wrong and he'd answer.

I held my breath as his phone rang until the familiar click and the sound of his voice invaded my senses. Without thinking, I pressed End and called him again. Voice mail answered each and every time.

I felt myself unraveling as my phone pinged again. The hand that held my phone was shaking so hard; it took me more than one try to touch the right place on my phone that would display the entire message.

TEXT ALERT UPDATE: Ryson Miller reportedly unresponsive in surfing accident in Malibu.

Unresponsive? What exactly does that mean? Where is he?

I needed to get to him, but how was I supposed to find

him? Where would he be brought? Tossing my phone on top of the desk, I attempted to focus, but tears blurred my vision. My throat felt thick as I searched for the nearest hospital on my laptop. The results popped up, and my phone pinged again. Dread filled my belly as I reached out for it, my heart plummeting in my chest.

TEXT ALERT UPDATE: RYSON MILLER REPORTEDLY DEAD AFTER SURFING ACCIDENT, AN EYEWITNESS VERIFIES. CONFIRMATION PENDING.

My cell phone dropped to the wood floor with a loud thud as all the air whooshed out of my lungs. I couldn't breathe. I couldn't see. I couldn't hear. I'd lost all ability to function as I crumbled to the ground next to my phone. We could lie in a broken heap together, me and my phone. Let the world find me here, cracked like my protective screen, broken like my phone case.

Ryson is dead?

Dead?

Dead?

Tears raced down my cheeks and splashed onto my bare legs. How did we have the ability to release so much water? My legs were drenched within minutes. I had to remind myself to breathe, to inhale. And then I wished it were all a hoax. People got bad information all the time.

Please be a hoax. Please be a hoax. Those four words became my silent motto.

My phone started ringing nonstop as the text messages and calls came in rapid-fire succession. There was no time to respond to one before ten more came in its place.

They all wanted to know the same thing I did.

Is it true? Could it be true? Is Ryson really dead? Am I okay?

When Ryson's mother called, I answered.

"Hi," I managed to squeak out.

"Quinn, please tell me he's with you. Please." Her voice broke as she sobbed against the receiver. "Please tell me he's there right now."

My throat felt like it was stuffed with cotton, and I gasped for anything that would help me breathe. Or let me die. In that moment, I wasn't sure which one I wanted more.

A sobbing, choking sound tore through me as I answered her question, "He's not here."

A feral scream ripped from her lungs, followed by a single word, "No." She ended the call before another word was spoken.

It was the most horrific sound I'd ever heard in my life, and I prayed I'd never hear anything like it again. Real pain wasn't something you could emulate or fake. Not even the best actors could pull it off. Not to that regard anyway. Real pain consumed you, shocked you, transformed you. It took your air and replaced it with something thick and unbreathable. It removed all of the color from your world. Suddenly, everything became black and white.

Shaking my head, I refused to believe that Ryson was gone. Wouldn't I have felt it if he died? Surely, the bond that connected us would have caused me physical pain the moment it was severed. I was convinced that I would know if he was dead; I would have felt something. And right now, I felt nothing. I was numb. A hollow shell.

"Quinn!" Paige's voice infiltrated my thoughts, but she sounded like a dream. "Quinn, where are you?"

"Office," I tried to shout, but it came out in a whisper instead.

The sound of Paige's footsteps racing through the house got louder the closer she got.

"Quinn!" she yelled before racing toward me. "Are you okay? Are you hurt?"

I looked at her face and knew she'd been crying. "No, I'm not okay," I answered.

She grabbed me by the shoulders. "We need to get to the hospital. He's not dead. Do you hear me?" she spoke the words slow and deliberate, but they did the trick.

I blinked rapidly. "What?"

"He's not dead. Get up," she demanded, sounding bossier than I'd ever heard her in my life.

"You're sure?"

"I'm sure. But we have to go." She tried to pull me up from the floor.

I wiped at my face, trying to dry my tears with my arms. "How do you know? How do you know and I don't?"

"Tatum and I were out, and the paparazzi were around. When the news broke, they told us. They have our reactions on film, Quinn. But one of the guys called his contacts at Santa Monica General, and they told him Ryson wasn't dead, but he was unconscious. He secretly let us know, and I came right over to get you. Tatum's at the hospital already. You weren't answering your phone and ..." Her voice faded out as my mind stopped processing any more words.

All I focused on was the fact that Ryson wasn't dead. He wasn't gone. He was still here, and I needed to get to him.

"We have to go. Now, Paige!" I practically yelled, and she nodded.

"Do you want to grab any clothes or anything?"

I had no idea what she meant. *Who cared about grabbing clothes at a time like this?*

"Just get me to Ryson. Please," I said as the tears continued to spill down my cheeks and my voice choked up with emotion.

"Let's go." We headed outside to her waiting car.

Paige opened the passenger door, and I slid in, going through the motions without thinking as my heart pounded so hard that I swore, you'd be able to see it trying to break out of my body. I glanced down at my chest just to make sure it was staying in place.

"It's going to be okay, Quinn. He's going to be okay." Paige sounded so soothing, so convinced of her lie that I almost agreed just to be agreeable. Almost.

"We don't know that," I said around the lump in my throat.

I needed to call Ryson's mom, but she'd ask me a million questions that I wouldn't have any answers to yet, so I typed out a quick text message instead, letting her know that Ryson was at Santa Monica General and that I was on my way there. For all I knew, they might have already called her, and she would be there before me. I sent a text message to my parents as well. They were still at work and most likely hadn't heard the news yet; otherwise, they would have reached out.

"Thank you for coming to get me." I could barely see our surroundings through my tears and knew there was no way I would have been able to navigate the roads without breaking down or causing an accident of my own.

"You'd do the same for me," she said before putting her hand on mine and giving it a squeeze.

The drive felt like it took a thousand hours. Nothing would have been fast enough for me. It could have taken us five whole minutes to get there, and it still would have been five minutes too long. Desperation pulled at me, its claws sinking into my skin and holding on tight. All I wanted to do was be there. Even though I knew there was nothing I could do, I still physically ached to be where Ryson was— occupying the same space, breathing the same air, waiting for news I had no control over.

We pulled into the emergency services parking lot, and I wondered why the hell so many cars filled the parking spots and none were empty. Were hospitals always this crowded? When we finally found a spot about a mile away, I barely remembered to grab my purse before I started sprinting at full speed toward the entrance doors. Paige shouted at me to stop, and I had almost forgotten she was even there.

The paparazzi were already outside, awaiting our arrival, and the camera flashes went off in rapid succession. They yelled my name and asked me questions, but nothing registered. Everything sounded like people screaming underwater, their voices unclear and muddy. Paige addressed them, but I had no idea what she'd said. My entire focus was getting the hell inside and closer to Ryson. I needed to know what was going on with him.

"I have to get to Ryson," I mumbled—or could have whispered.

The automatic doors swung open, and Paige ushered me through them, her hand firmly on my lower back.

The bright lights of the waiting room hit me at full force, and I realized just how blurry my vision truly was. I swiped at my eyes with the back of my hand, but it was no use. Looking around, I scanned the area, searching for the check-in desk, an information desk, or anything useful.

"Quinn."

I turned and saw Tatum walking toward us.

"Go talk to someone at the window right there," he said, pointing. "They won't tell me shit." He possessively wrapped an arm around Paige.

Nodding, I did what Tatum had told me. I stood at the window and waited. There was no one in there. Lifting my hand, I started knocking against the glass, my raps on it growing quicker and more frantic until a face finally appeared.

"Can I help you?" she asked as she slid open the glass partition separating us, only mildly annoyed.

"Yes. My boyfriend. They brought my boyfriend in, and I don't know if he's okay," I said, my hands shaking as the tears splashed onto the countertop.

"His name?" She looked at me, her fingers poised on top

of the computer keyboard as I told her his full name and she began typing it in. I waited as she read the screen before saying, "You'll have to take a seat, please. I can't tell you anything."

"You can't? Is there anyone I can talk to who knows something? Please? Anything at all," I begged. The voice coming out of me sounded like something I didn't even recognize.

"The doctor will be out to talk to you as soon as they have any news. But for now, the best thing you can do for your boyfriend is remain calm, pray—if you believe in that— and wait. I'm sorry, but that's all the information I have."

"The doctor? Is he in surgery? Just shake your head yes or no, please," I continued pleading and she nodded.

I thanked her before looking around for Paige and Tatum, finding them in the corner, far away as possible from the rest of the people in the room. There were a fair number of people in here, and I wondered if they were all waiting on news of their loved ones the same way I was. *How many walked through these doors each day and night, their hearts in a state of flux, waiting on news?* It was something I'd never thought about before, but now, I was obsessed. This was an everyday occurrence for a hospital—life and death, people's days either made or destroyed ... lives completely altered in moments.

"What'd they say?" Tatum asked as I sat next to him.

"She won't tell me anything, but I got it out of her that he's in surgery. But that's all I know."

"Your phone keeps ringing, Quinn," Paige said as she

handed me my clutch, which I'd shoved at Tatum without realizing it.

My phone? I looked at the clutch in her hand and felt confused. I'd brought it with us? *Why wasn't my brain working right? Why couldn't I remember the simplest things?* Reaching inside, I pulled out my phone, which was filled with notifications of every kind. Scrolling through my missed calls, I stopped on Madison's name. I pressed dial.

"Quinn? Is it true? Where are you?"

"It's true. Paige brought me. We're at Santa Monica General. You have to get here."

"We're on our way," she said before ending the call.

Looking at Paige and Tatum, I said, "Madison. I forgot to call her." I felt bad.

"She understands," Paige said. "Are they on their way?"

"Yeah."

"Good," she said before focusing on the door. "Ryson's mom's here."

My head snapped toward the entrance, and I instantly spotted her. I got to my feet and walked in a rushed pace toward her. She looked frantic, her dark hair sticking out in places and her face tear-streaked.

"Quinn!" she said before wrapping me in a hug. "What happened?"

"I don't know. They won't tell me anything specific. He left to go surfing, but that's all I know."

"I'm going to get some damn answers." She sounded determined and scared.

I let go of her hand before watching her head toward the

same window I'd just been at. She started knocking the same way I had only moments ago, and I slowly found my way back to Paige and Tatum.

I had no idea how much time had passed, but the commotion and yelling of the paparazzi alerted me to the fact that Madison and Walker had arrived. It was a celebrity-filled hospital, but the best part was that no one in the waiting room seemed to care. And if they did, they sure as hell didn't act like it. I was grateful for the privacy. And grateful for my friends.

When Ryson's mom came back, she hugged everyone in greeting before filling us all in. "It was an actual surfing accident. I don't know why I thought he was in a car accident. I think I read the word accident." Her eyes met mine as she continued, "And I guess I just assumed. But it happened in the water. Some sort of collision between him and another surfer. He lost consciousness, so I'm presuming he hit his head, but that's just a guess because he is in surgery right now and has been since he arrived."

It was a little more than I had known, more than they had told me, even though it still wasn't very much.

"That doesn't sound so bad, right?" Madison spoke up, her voice hopeful.

"Yeah, I mean, how bad can a surfing accident really be?" Paige asked, her tone mimicking Madison's, but it was the complete opposite of how I felt.

"Bad enough that he's in the hospital, having surgery, and people thought he was dead," Walker said grimly, bringing the reality crashing back.

"They thought that because he was unconscious though, right?" Tatum added, trying to sound neutral and composed.

"I'm not trying to be a downer," Walker said, his voice collected, "but I don't want you to think that it's no big deal. People die in surfing accidents. You can drown. Your body crashes into things. You get head trauma. You break bones. You're the water's bitch, and it's not the other way around."

"Jeez, babe," Madison said before giving him a look.

"I'm sorry. I just ..." Walker paused. "I'm just being realistic, and I'm worried, okay?"

Ryson's mom squeezed my hand tight as she said, "We all are, but he's strong. He's going to make it. I know it. I can feel it."

She gave me a soft smile, and I wanted to give her one in return, but my lips refused to cooperate. I couldn't pretend that everything was okay when it wasn't. And until I knew for sure exactly what was going on, I stayed in emotional limbo.

FALLING FOR HIM

THE PAST

Quinn

I'D OVERHEARD RYSON mention something in passing last week about surfing and how he'd taken it up again. It never occurred to me that he could even surf. Then, I remembered a movie where he'd played a surfer, and my blood started to stir. Intrigued and a little turned on, I'd asked him for more information about it because, truth be told, I'd always loved the beach, the ocean, and definitely the surfers who navigated the ocean like it belonged to them. What red-blooded Southern California girl didn't? Anyone who told you otherwise was a filthy, dirty liar.

It was my dream to live in Malibu one day, and the idea of watching Ryson surf there lit a small fire inside me. I imagined us waking up in the morning together before I walked onto our balcony and saw him hit the waves.

I shook my head to come back to reality. I was way too young to be planning out my entire future, and Ryson was currently a tornado with the potential to decimate everything in his path.

Still, I couldn't stop myself from trying to find out exactly where he surfed. I'd badgered him about it until he finally relented and gave up his secret.

"Surfrider," he'd said.

I'd smiled in response. It was one of my three favorite beaches in Malibu, and it suited him even though I knew the local surf gods there tended to give outsiders a hard time.

I would head to Point Dume whenever I wanted to view the dolphins or relax without any fanfare. Zuma was great for people-watching and surfers of all ages, and it usually had pretty thick crowds. It was definitely harder to go unnoticed there, so it was the one I frequented the least, but I still had a soft spot for it. And Surfrider was where the old-school surfers hung out. Their attitudes flared and tempers raged as they claimed that stretch of sea as their own. Me, I just liked to sit in the sand and observe them weave in and out of the waves like they had been born on them. It fascinated me, the way the boards looked like an extension of their bodies, cutting through the water at their command.

That was why I was currently sitting in the small parking lot at half past five in the morning, watching Ryson zip up his black pant wetsuit and run toward the sea, surfboard tucked under his arm. He moved the board to the front of his body as he leaped into the ocean, and my body shook involuntarily in response as I imagined the chills that must have run through him. That water wasn't even remotely warm, and even with a wetsuit on, you could still feel the cold all the way down to your bones.

Ryson paddled out, and I knew that I'd lose sight of him soon if I didn't get out of my car and head toward the sand. I'd been watching him surf here for the past four mornings in a row, thankful that he seemed to stick to a routine. I wasn't sure if he knew I was there or not since I always bolted before he came back to shore. I knew it seemed like a creepy thing to do—observe him without his knowledge—but it felt necessary, almost like I didn't have a choice in the matter. Wherever Ryson was, my body followed.

Grabbing a blanket from my car, I wrapped it around my body as I made my way through the semi-darkness and onto the cold sand. Ryson wasn't alone, but he was easy to pick out. He sat up straighter and looked taller than the other guys perched on their boards. His shoulders weren't as broad, but I could pick that body out of a silhouetted lineup if I had to. I imagined how it felt to sit on top of the water, rolling back and forth with the current, and hoped that Ryson felt as calm and as peaceful as he seemed to look.

When a wave started to form to the right, I saw the small group all paddle toward it, each one vying for a piece of the ocean to claim as their own, if only for a moment. Ryson crouched on his board before rising higher. One foot in front of the other, he controlled it perfectly, slapping the front down and maneuvering it with the current. He weaved in and out, riding until the wave resembled little more than a splash in a pool, and he collapsed on top of his board with a thud, the droplets spraying around him before he turned around and paddled right back out.

I could watch him all day. I wanted to. But the sun was

rising, we needed to be on set in a few hours, and I didn't want Ryson to catch me spying on him like some stalker. Bundled up in my blanket, I made my way toward my car and drove off without saying a word, just like I'd done every morning this week.

WAITING ROOM HELL
THE PRESENT
Quinn

MY PARENTS SHOWED up, the two of them frantic until their eyes landed on the group of us in the corner. They hugged me hard, sitting with Ryson's mom and catching up. They were both teachers, in the middle of exam season, and when it came time for them to leave, as much as it pained them to go, I told them that I'd call them as soon as we had any news. Besides, I knew they'd be back, whether I asked them to or not. My parents loved Ryson like a son.

It felt like we had been in that waiting room for days, the six of us collectively holding our breaths, sitting on chairs that had grown far too uncomfortable as we waited for the doctor to come out and give us any kind of news. Of course, it had only been a few hours, but during those moments when you had no answers, time seemed to stand still. A thousand questions flooded my head, spinning and turning like a pinwheel in the wind. And in the spaces between all the madness lay hope.

Hope that this was all a nightmare we would wake up from.

Hope that he would be okay.

Hope that he would pull through.

I'd been unable to breathe right since the moment I first read the news. Nothing worked properly inside of me anymore. My internal organs paused, waiting on whether or not they would be allowed to continue working as normal or if they'd have to find a new way to do their job. My heart waited as well to figure out if it would be forced to shatter beyond repair or be allowed to remain intact. Everything in me was waiting.

I did a lot of bargaining in that room. I would do anything to make sure Ryson got through this in one piece and came home to me again. And as I glanced around at the people sitting next to me, I knew I wasn't the only one. You see, nothing in life prepared you for what it felt like to sit in an emergency room. To not know if the person you loved would live or die was a special kind of hell beyond all words, reason, or description. It could only be experienced.

The doctor emerged, charging straight for us as he removed his surgical cap and folded it into his hands. We all stood as he neared. My lower back ached in places I hadn't realized were sore.

"Ryson pulled through surgery," he said.

My lungs instantly inflated, and my heart thankfully started sputtering back to life.

"He has a lot of swelling on his brain from the force of the impact. He's in a medically induced coma right now."

My voice cracked as I asked, "What does that mean?"

"It just means that we have him sedated until his brain gets back down to normal levels. Then, we'll slowly bring him out and see if there is any other damage."

"What kind of damage?" Ryson's mom asked as she wiped a stray tear from her cheek.

I'd never seen her cry before, and I remembered Ryson telling me how he had never once seen her cry either.

"Speech impediment. Physical function. Motor skills," he listed them off before continuing, "We want to make sure he's okay, but we won't actually know until he wakes up."

"How long will that be? When will he wake up?" she asked, and her pained voice caused my heart to ache.

"There's no way of knowing. These things take time, and every case is unique. It could be hours. Or it could be days. In rare cases, even longer."

The doctor refused to give us specifics because he didn't have them. And in this sue-happy country we'd somehow created, he was probably only allowed to speak in generics. Anything else, and he'd get the hospital in trouble. I wanted to scream at him, shake him, and make him tell us more, but I knew he wouldn't.

"What do you recommend we do?" Madison asked, and I realized just how amazing she was under pressure.

"Go home. Rest. But I'm sure none of you will do that, so I'll just make sure to tell you to eat. People always forget to eat," he said with a small smile before asking, "Any more questions before I head back?"

Everyone looked between me and Ryson's mom.

"I don't think so," she said.

The doctor gave us a curt nod before turning to walk away.

"Wait," I shouted at his retreating back, and he immediately stopped moving. "Do you know where his things are? Did he come in with anything?"

The doctor slowly shook his head. "No, there were no personal belongings on him. Just his person."

"Shit," I said out loud, suddenly nervous. That meant that Ryson's cell phone was out there somewhere, and absolutely anyone could have it. There were personal things on that phone—pictures, text messages, emails, phone numbers. "His cell."

"Can you track it?" Walker asked.

I nodded, forgetting completely that I could do just that. I pulled up the app and let it run, the location pinpoint appearing within seconds.

"It says it's still on the beach. I can't believe it. Can someone go get it?" I said, starting to freak out.

If the paparazzi or a fan got ahold of Ryson's phone, who knew what they'd do with it? Even though his phone was protected with a passcode, I knew that that was no dissuasion for thieves and hackers. Everything had a price in this town, and this would absolutely be no exception. I couldn't even think about that right now.

"Tatum and I will go," Walker said before he looked at Tatum, who nodded in agreement. "Let us know if the location moves or anything."

"Thanks, you guys."

"Of course. We'd do anything for you two," they both said before giving their respective girlfriends a kiss and heading out the main door toward the waiting onslaught of reporters and the growing group of fans.

Paige started pacing back and forth, and I knew she was dying to feel useful. "Do you want me and Madison to go get you a change of clothes or some food or something?"

I nodded. "I think an overnight bag might be good. And some clothes for Ryson too." When he finally woke up, he'd need something to wear. "Just grab him a pair of shorts and a pair of joggers. A couple of shirts and a hoodie. Is that okay? Is that too much?"

"No. It's perfect. He needs options," Paige said reassuringly. She was literally the kindest person I knew. All the fame hadn't changed her at all.

"We'll be back. Do you need anything, Mrs. Miller?" Madison asked Ryson's mom.

She shook her head, her dark hair swishing back and forth.

The buzz of the paparazzi roared to life each time my friends stepped outside, but the ruckus died down just as quickly soon after they left. I was worried they might follow the guys to the beach and actually beat them to Ryson's things, but as far as I could tell, none of them were following my friends. They stayed firmly camped outside.

As long as Ryson was in a coma, his condition still undetermined, it was good for business. Nothing garnered more web hits, clicks, and publicity than a critically injured celebrity. The next best thing was a grieving girlfriend. I knew the truth was that they were all out there, waiting for me. I was their meal ticket. My pain was their profit. But they wouldn't be getting anything from me today or anytime soon. They could fucking starve to death for all I cared.

★ ★ ★

TATUM AND WALKER returned with Ryson's phone way before the girls got back with my things.

"You found it," I said, breathing out with relief as they handed me his phone and a black duffel bag. I quickly unlocked his phone and made sure it was his before pressing it against my chest.

"Thank God," Ryson's mom said from her seat. She had been sitting as long as I'd been pacing.

"It was there. We even found his surfboard. It was lying in the sand away from all of his other shit," Walker said before apologizing to Ryson's mom for swearing, who waved him off. She'd heard it all before.

"I can't believe it," I said, still shocked. "I can't believe it was all sitting there."

"I know. They must have thought it was someone's stuff who was still in the water," Walker said, meaning that the other surfers at the beach hadn't touched it because they thought the owner was still around, surfing with them. His things would have started gathering suspicion and most likely not lasted long after the sun started to set and the water cleared out.

"It was almost too good to be true," Tatum said. "His

surfboard's in the back of my truck, but I'll drop it off at your place later, okay?"

"Thank you."

Walker took a step toward me before nodding at the glass doors behind us. "You know, there're a lot of people out there."

"I know," I said.

Walker shook his head as if I didn't understand. "No, you don't. It's not just reporters. There're a lot of fans. They're holding vigils. They have signs. They're crying."

I looked in the direction of the doors and actually took notice of the size of the crowd that had gathered. I had no idea how I hadn't really seen it before—all the teenagers and homemade signs that looked like something you'd bring to a concert for your favorite band. "Do you think I should go out there and say something?"

Walker offered a quick nod. "Probably. But wait for Madison. She'll know exactly what to do," he said, and I agreed.

Madison was my new agent after all, and this was something I wouldn't do without her opinion. No sooner did the thought cross my mind than the doors whooshed open again, and the crowd roared, screaming Paige's name. My two best friends walked inside, their heads focused on the ground to avoid the camera flashes.

Paige handed me an oversize bag. "There're clothes and makeup and a brush and stuff. I didn't know how long you'd be here, but I planned ahead."

"Thank you," I said before giving her a hug.

"And we brought your car, so you'd have it," Madison said as she navigated my body away from the prying eyes outside. "Has anyone told you that it's a madhouse out there?"

"Yeah. Your boyfriend did. Do you think I should go say something? How should we handle this?" I looked at her with pleading eyes.

She sucked in a breath before addressing Ryson's mom, "If you're comfortable with it, I think you should be the one to give them a general update on Ryson's condition. It would be nice to have it come from you since he's your son."

His mom nodded, agreeing with the sentiment. "I'm comfortable with that."

"Good. Okay," Madison said before directing her attention toward me. "Um, my only issue is that all those people out there would rather hear from and see you, Quinn," she said with an uncomfortable laugh. "No offense, Mrs. Miller."

"None taken." Ryson's mom offered a small smile. "I know how this industry operates."

"Does Quinn have to talk?" Tatum questioned, still clearly trying to learn the ins and outs of this business and our place in it.

Madison looked at him as she explained, "Well, it's just that Quinn and Ryson are a package deal. You don't think about one of them without thinking about the other. They've been together for years. They live together. It's just the way it is with the two of them. So, yeah, it would be weird if Quinn didn't talk to the press at all."

"I agree," I said easily because she was right. "But what

am I saying exactly?"

"I think you should go out there and basically thank everyone for coming. There are so many fans out there. Tell them it means a lot to you that they care and that they're praying for Ryson. You're grateful for their support. That kind of thing."

I nodded, liking the plan, but I had just one more stipulation to add. "Will you all come out with us? In case I lose my voice or start crying or something. I'd like it best if we all went together," I said, realizing how much I needed their support.

"Yes! Of course," the group announced in unison, talking over one another.

I couldn't stop the emotion from spilling over. Allowing a few grateful tears to fall, I wiped them away before smoothing out my shirt and hair.

"Madison," I said as I reached for her shoulder, "who should talk first?"

"Mrs. Miller should go first with the update. And then you can thank everyone, and we'll end with that."

Sucking in a deep, steadying breath, I announced, "Okay. I'm ready. Let's go." Reaching for Mrs. Miller's hand, I held it tight as the six of us walked outside together, a unified force.

The clicking of the cameras and questions being hurled from all sides inundated us the moment we stepped out of the air-conditioned room and into the Southern California heat. Within seconds, all the shouting stopped, as Madison stood at the forefront, her hand held high in the air as everyone stopped talking. It grew eerily quiet, except for the sound of cameras clicking and a few whispers.

"Hello. I'm Madison Myers, Ryson Miller and Quinn Johnson's agent. Ryson's mother Lynnette and Quinn will be giving short statements, but we will not be answering any questions at this time."

"Mrs. Miller?" Madison reached for Ryson's mom and pulled her toward the front.

"Wow, this is a bit overwhelming. There are so many of you," she said, sounding absolutely controlled. "Right now, we don't have much of an update, but we can tell you this. Ryson is out of surgery, but he's in a medically induced coma. He has swelling on his brain, and we won't know anything more until he wakes up."

She took a step back, her eyes searching for mine, and I smiled before taking her place.

"Hi, everyone. I'm Quinn Johnson, Ryson Miller's girl-friend." My voice caught, and I cleared my throat as I noticed the sheer number of devices recording my every move. Of course they all knew who I was, but I wasn't in my right state of mind. "I just wanted to thank you so much for coming out here and for all your prayers and support," I said, looking directly at the group of fans who were watching me speak with tears in their eyes. "It means a lot that you care so much. You have no idea. Please keep Ryson—" My voice suddenly broke, and I lost it. I tried to find my voice again but couldn't. My vision blurred as tears spilled. I attempted once more to speak, but nothing came out, and I buried my head in Mrs. Miller's shoulder as the sound of shutter clicks filled my ears.

Madison stepped forward and handled things like the professional she was. "That's all we know for now. Thank you again for coming. Please keep Ryson, his mother, and Quinn in your thoughts."

The six of us turned around and walked into the hospital together as the shouting started back up and rose to levels that were unimaginable. They wanted answers we didn't have. They wanted pieces of us we couldn't give. We'd already told them everything we knew. And I'd already given them more than I'd intended.

They were going to have a field day with my breakdown.

TEENAGE NIGHTMARE
THE PAST
Quinn

R YSON STOPPED DOING whatever it was that he had been doing. Or at least he was attempting too. I don't think he even realized how truly addicted he was until he started behaving oddly during one of our most playful scenes. We were supposed to be flirting while he pushed me on a swing, but instead of him smiling and being sweet, Ryson's expression looked pained, unnatural even, as my body flew back and forth through the air.

"Cut," the director yelled, massaging her temples with two fingers as she glared at us. "Ryson, you're supposed to be happy in this scene. You're flirting, having fun. Stop looking like your dog just died."

I twisted my body around in the swing, so I could get a good look at him, and that was when I noticed the beads of sweat covering his brow. His body shook slightly and if you weren't paying attention, you wouldn't see it, but I caught it.

Overcome with an intense desire to help fix him, I asked

the director, "I'm sorry, but can I borrow him really quick? We'll be right back, I promise."

I waited for her okay before I hopped off the swing and reached for Ryson's hand. Pulling him through the stage doors, I shushed him until we were in private. I led him straight into my trailer and closed the door tight behind us.

"What's going on?" I asked in a sympathetic voice as I closed the windows as well, not wanting any unwelcome ears to overhear our conversation.

Hundreds of people worked on a movie set at any given time, and signing nondisclosure agreements never stopped them from *anonymously* reporting things to the press for money during filming or once we wrapped. The last thing I wanted was to give anyone ammunition to use against Ryson and cause him more pain, when it was so clear that he was already hurting.

"What do you mean?" he asked before wiping at his forehead.

"Why are you shaking and sweating at the same time? Are you cold? Are you hot? What is it? Are you sick?" I knew I sounded a little crazed, hurling my questions at him before I could take another breath, but I wasn't an expert on drugs, and my knowledge was extremely limited. I'd never felt more naive than I did in this moment.

He shifted on his feet before looking around and sitting at my reading table. "I'm not sick. You know how hot the lights are. They always make me sweat."

I sat down across from him, nodding in agreement about the lights. They were damn hot at times, but that wasn't it, and I pieced together exactly what was happening. "Ryson, I think I know what you're trying to do."

"And what's that?" He tried to act coy, but his shoulders started shaking as he avoided eye contact with me.

"You stopped using. Am I right?"

He swallowed hard, and I watched while his Adam's apple bobbed up and down in this throat as he swallowed hard. He nodded, and I wanted to crawl across the table, take this guy into my arms, hold him tight, and never let go. What was it about a guy in pain that made a girl want to save him?

"I love that you're trying to get clean right now. But it's not working," I said softly, my brain feeling like it was splitting in two. I had no idea what to do or how to fix this without ruining our entire shoot.

"No better time than the present," he tried to joke as he wiped the sweat from his forehead with the back of his hand once more.

I looked him dead in the eyes. "Ryson, look at me," I demanded and waited for his brown eyes to meet mine. "You can't do this by yourself, and you shouldn't be alone. They'll never use these scenes in the final cut. They aren't good enough," I added, hoping it would get him to see reason. If I took the focus off of him personally and put it onto work and the fact that none of these scenes would end up in the actual movie, maybe he'd understand.

"I'm not alone, Quinn. I have you."

He reached across for my hand, but I pulled it away from his grasp even though the gesture killed me. He would take the movement as a rejection even though it wasn't at all how

I meant it.

"I'm not equipped to deal with this kind of thing. I don't know what to do." I knew my words came out sounding angry, but I felt helpless as I smacked my palms on top of the table out of frustration and fear.

"Then, what are you saying exactly? What are we doing in here? Why did you pull us away?" He looked around like he was utterly confused.

"I'm saying that you need help. You need a professional, Ryson. You can't be like this for the next three weeks. It's not going to work."

"Three more weeks," he said, his voice sounding distant. The wheels in his head were spinning—that much I could tell, but I couldn't tell anything else. "You're right; I can't."

I blew out a soft breath. "What are you thinking?"

"I feel like shit, Quinn," he admitted, and I knew he was telling the truth.

"I know you do."

"I don't think I can quit cold turkey." The front of his hair was wet. His shoulders slumped forward as he put his head in his hands. "I'm so sorry. I tried. I tried to stop," he said, his voice muffled.

My mind reeled, taking me places in the past I normally refused to go but it was too late. My innocence played out in front of me as I started to get emotional. "Please, Ryson. Please don't die on me."

His head lifted from his hands as his eyes pulled together. "Why would I die on you?" He huffed out a small laugh like it was some kind of joke before his demeanor shifted again.

"Shit. You were there when Sissy died, weren't you? I'm sorry, Quinn. I completely forgot about that."

Ryson reached out and placed a clammy hand on top of mine. This time, I didn't move out of his grasp.

I had only been twelve years old when I was cast as Sissy Turner's younger sister. I had idolized her on and off the screen since the first time I'd seen her on a popular television show. I remembered thinking how this role with her would be my big break and how I'd looked forward to learning everything she would allow me to. I planned on following her around like a real little sister would until she made me stop.

Sissy overdosed in her trailer and died during a fifteen-minute break for lighting adjustments. Fifteen minutes. That was all it had taken to lose a life.

The movie, which was highly anticipated and had garnered talk for awards season, was scrapped completely. Management briefly considered a recast, but everyone claimed that they were too devastated to go on and that no one could replace Sissy. I had never before been in a movie that was simply thrown away like that, and I had worked my ass off to secure that coveted role.

"It was awful. And then they threw the movie out, like it never even existed. Like she never existed." I shook my head at the memories and glanced down at our clasped hands, willing history to not repeat itself.

If Ryson died, they'd probably throw away this movie, too, and I'd be known as the girl who killed her castmates or some other screwed-up headline that would sell more magazines in the supermarket. They'd label me cursed, and people who used to be my friends would refuse to work with me.

The entire fake future scenario played out in my head until Ryson spoke again, breaking me out of my thoughts, "I remember that too. I always thought it was really messed up that they'd canned the whole project instead of recasting." His thumb rubbed circles on top of my hand.

"Well, production schedules, time, money, and all that. You know how it is." I fought back the tears as I rolled my eyes and removed my hand from his. His touch weakened me to the real reason we were sitting in my trailer.

"I do know. I don't want this project shelved, and I don't want to be recast. It would break my fucking heart to see you with another love interest."

"Why?"

"You know why." He tried to sound flirtatious, but it was half-assed at best, and he looked worse than he had just five minutes prior. "I promise, I won't die on you. I have an idea, but I'm not sure you're going to like it." His face lit up.

"I'm all ears."

A loud knock on the door scared me half to death as a production assistant shouted our names. "They need you both back on set!"

"Tell her we just need five more minutes." I responded for the both of us.

I heard the PA audibly groan as she walked away, mumbling something about how she wasn't going to get yelled at for us.

I looked back at Ryson. "You were saying?"

"I'll just do a tiny little bit to get by."

"What do you mean?"

"Obviously, I can't just quit. You said it's not working. So, I'll just do a little bit to take the edge off. Deal?"

He was asking me for permission that I had absolutely no right to give. I was in over my head, and Ryson sensed my hesitation.

"Quinn, if you tell them, they'll postpone production for who knows how long. What if they decide they can't wait and they fire me? What if I can't get better in time to continue filming? Then, what happens? I just want to finish this with you, and then I promise on my mom's life that I'll check into rehab and get help. I swear to you. Just let me get through the next few weeks, and then I'll be the man you deserve. Please don't give up on me yet."

He was trying to scare me with reality and appeal to my heart at the same time. And it worked.

"I have one condition," I started to say, my voice shaking as I prayed to God I was doing the right thing.

He waved a hand. "Let me hear it."

Looking down, I tried to formulate my thoughts perfectly before I talked. I'd realized early on that this business wasn't personal and that the majority of people on set didn't give two shits about my well-being even if they pretended to.

Fearing that they would encourage Ryson to do whatever he needed to finish this shoot on time and on budget, I made a vow to keep his problem to myself for now as long as he seemed in some kind of control. We only had each other, and

I convinced myself that I was doing the right thing.

"If I think you're not okay for even one second, I'll tell someone. I'll be the one who stops production, and we're going to get you help." I swallowed around the lump in my throat. "I will not lose you, Ryson Miller, and this movie is not more important than your life."

"You'll never lose me, Quinn. Once I have you, I'm never leaving your side. Hope you don't plan on getting tired of me, you know, for the rest of your life."

He raised his eyebrows, and I actually managed a laugh.

"You agree to my condition then?"

"I do."

I knew that I was enabling Ryson by not forcing him to get help immediately or by not saying something to an adult, but in the past, the adults were usually the ones who provided the drugs in the first place. Who was to say that this situation wouldn't have the same results?

The truth was that I didn't trust people to do the right thing. I'd seen it so many times over and over again. Ever since the incident when I was ten, I'd stopped believing that people in power positions had any good intentions outside of their own agenda. They would probably ply Ryson with more than he needed just to get him to finish shooting on time. Everything boiled down to money. There was a thick river of greed that ran through this town, the bridges that crossed them built on ego. It was as dysfunctional as it was expected.

"You promise you'll help me after we're done though? You won't leave me behind the second we wrap?"

His dark eyes met mine, and I fought off the overwhelming urge to press my lips to his and give him my heart right then and there.

"I won't leave you. I'll help you. Okay?" The words were a promise. A promise I wouldn't break if we made it through this shoot in one piece.

We were playing hardball with Ryson's life, and I hoped like hell we weren't making a mistake.

WAITING GAME
THE PRESENT
Quinn

EIGHT DAYS LATER, Ryson's condition still hadn't changed. He was comatose, his brain still swollen, but he was showing signs of improvement, albeit slowly.

The doctors had tried to get us to go home, insisting that they would call the second anything changed, but I refused to leave Ryson's side.

His mom, however, had decided to go back to work part-time. Her clients had been routed to other psychiatrists, but they still called, texted, and left crying voice mails, telling her that they needed to see her. She felt torn in her obligations. I sensed it but didn't make her feel badly about it. There was nothing she could do for Ryson anyway, so I didn't blame her for leaving to help the people she could actually help.

Plus, I could tell that she craved some normalcy. It was just that, for me, nothing would be normal again until Ryson woke up. I couldn't go home, to the house we shared, without him. I knew that I'd hate every second of being away from him if I didn't have to be, so I didn't.

And when the staff had tried to gently tell me that visiting hours were over on that first night, I'd informed them that I wasn't a visitor and that I wouldn't be leaving. Being a famous actress might have helped me out a little because they'd relented and allowed me to stay, never asking me to leave again.

If the situation were reversed, I knew beyond a shadow of a doubt that Ryson would never leave my side. He'd fight the doctors, the nurses, and the security staff to stay with me. That was how fiercely he loved me. And that was how I chose to love him in return. No one and nothing would tear us apart.

In his private room, I'd moved the recliner next to his bed, and I'd been sleeping there, holding his hand in mine each night.

"Still nothing?" Ryson's mom popped her head in and smiled at me as she quietly closed the door.

"No," I said with a slow shake.

"You sure you don't want to go home, sweetie? I'll stay with him tonight," she offered, knowing that I would refuse.

"It's okay. I can't go home to our bed and sleep there without him anyway. Not like this," I said.

She gave me a sympathetic look. "I understand."

I sucked in a long breath before admitting, "We were fighting that day." Tears filled my eyes. "I was really mad at him when he left to go surfing."

She moved into the additional chair on the other side of

Ryson's hospital bed. "What were you guys fighting about?"

I looked into her brown eyes, the same color as his, as she waited for my response. She looked so tired.

"About getting married. It seems so stupid now," I said, shaking my head.

It did seem dumb to be fighting over that while he was lying in this bed, his brain so swollen that he wasn't allowed to wake up.

Her face pinched together as if the topic were completely foreign to her. "What about getting married?"

"Ryson doesn't want to," I said matter-of-factly, assuming she already knew this information about her only son.

"He doesn't? He actually said that?" She looked more confused than ever.

"Yeah." A soft laugh escaped. "It's, like, literally the one thing we fight over."

She looked down at her son and rubbed his shoulder. "Oh, Ryson," she said his name, sounding so sad. "I had no idea."

"Really? He never told you?"

"I guess I never asked before. I always just assumed that, of course, you two would get married," she said with a shrug.

"I always did too. Until we talked about it once. And he said that he didn't believe in it and he didn't see the point."

"Oh, Quinn, I'm so sorry. I'm sure he didn't really mean that."

"It doesn't matter." I started to cry. "I hate myself for fighting with him, and now, he's here, like this." I waved my hand over his sleeping body. "What if he never wakes up? I was so mad at him when he left, so angry that he was leaving me when we weren't in a good place."

"Don't do that to yourself," she started to say before clearing her throat. Her tone grew strong and clear. "This isn't your fault. He's going to wake up. And it's all going to be okay. Trust me, my son knows how much you love him. That is one thing he tells me all the time even though he doesn't have to. I see it whenever I'm with the two of you."

The tears fell harder. I was an emotional wreck, thinking back at how cold I had been to him when he left the house. How I turned my back after he told me he loved me, not wanting to look at him anymore. Even though I told him that I loved him back, my tone was annoyed and irritated. I said it that way on purpose. I wanted him to know I was upset, to send a message that we still weren't okay. And I wrongfully assumed that I could still be mad at him later that night when he finally came back home. Only he hadn't come back.

"Thank you for that," I said, trying to sound grateful.

"I mean it, sweetheart. Thank you for loving him the way you do. I'm not sure I ever told you that before, but I always meant to."

I knew she was only trying to make me feel better, but I didn't want to. I wanted to punish myself because the man I loved was sitting in a hospital bed, unable to open his eyes. And if I had just been straightforward and told him that I didn't want him to go surfing until we fixed things between us, he wouldn't be here. He'd be at home, with me, laughing and loving and planning that damn reality show he had been so excited about. He'd be talking about the next step in our lives, not sitting here, fighting for his.

THIS HAPPENS SOMETIMES
Quinn

OUR FRIENDS STOPPED by the hospital every single day, and even though they felt as helpless as I did, nothing was going to prevent them from coming. It was one thing for me to be strong, but even the strongest person needed to lean on others sometimes. I'd never realized it before because I always had Ryson. He was my rock, my go-to, the glue that held me together if I ever felt the need to fall apart. The four of them made me realize that I wasn't alone, and for that, I was eternally grateful.

Paige and Madison had tried once to get me to go home overnight. They'd suggested a sleepover, but I'd only had to tell them both *no* one time before they got the message and never asked again. We all knew that if it was either one of their boyfriends lying in that bed, they wouldn't leave either. There was a level of understanding between us three girls that gave me comfort. I didn't have to try to explain myself with words or attempt to get them to see my point of view or understand how I felt.

They all felt the exact same way for their men.

"Good evening, everyone." Ryson's on-call doctor walked into the room, wearing a smile I'd never seen before across his face. "Today's the day," he announced.

I sat up extra tall, my eyes boring into his as the nurse padded in behind him, writing notes on her clipboard.

"The swelling is gone?"

"It's gone down enough for us to bring him out. It can take time though, so don't worry if he doesn't wake up right away. Most people usually don't," he said as he moved toward the tubes attached to Ryson and inserted some sort of clear liquid into one.

We all collectively held our breath as we stared at Ryson's face, assuming he would open his eyes even though the doctor had said it didn't work that way. There was no reasoning when it came to your heart and what it wanted. It hoped in its own way, wanting reality to defy all rules and break all boundaries.

When over an hour had passed and Ryson still hadn't stirred, the room cleared out for the night, leaving me alone with him.

"I love you. I hope you wake up soon," I whispered into his ear before placing a kiss on his forehead.

It was an incredible thing to miss someone you could still look at and see. Ryson was right there in front of me, yet I ached for him in ways I'd never known were possible.

Sitting down in my familiar chair, I pulled a blanket over my body and gripped his hand in mine as I closed my eyes, falling into a deep sleep quicker than I had anticipated.

Jerking movements eventually pulled me from my

dreams. I opened my eyes at the same time that a hand intermittently squeezed mine. At first, I thought I was imagining it, but the light squeezes continued, practically keeping time with my beating heart.

"Ryson?" I asked, rubbing my eyes and trying to focus on his face, but it was too dark in the room to see him or anything clearly. I stood up and switched on a light. "Oh my gosh, Ryson?"

His eyes were open, and my heart started pounding, the beats hard and swift. I rushed to the side of his bed, tears flooding my eyes as my fingers brushed through his hair.

"Ryson? Can you hear me?"

He still hadn't said anything, and his expression seemed off, confused even, like he wasn't quite sure where he was.

"Why do you keep saying that word?" His voice was raspy and strained.

"What word?" I asked as concern flooded my veins.

"Ryson."

The smile I wore instantly dropped as I looked into his dark brown eyes. "Because it's your name."

"Oh." His eyebrows pulled together.

"You don't know your name?" I asked.

He shrugged, the movement slow. "I'm not sure," he said, his speech sluggish and raspy even though he still sounded like the Ryson I knew and loved. "Who are you?"

"Wait, what?" I practically tripped on the words, my mind unable to believe what he was asking. "You don't know—" I started to say, but the on-call doctor walked in and interrupted.

"You're awake! That's great news," the doctor said, his eyes bright and cheery as he looked between both me and Ryson with a smile on his face.

"He doesn't know who I am," I said through my shock as my stomach nervously twisted.

I'd stayed so strong throughout all of this, holding myself together and telling myself that everything would be fine once he woke up. I willed Ryson to wake up, knowing the world would continue spinning on its axis again once he did. That was all I wanted, all I asked for, all I thought I needed—for him to open his eyes and come back to me. I never once considered or even thought that he wouldn't know who I was once he did. It'd never occurred to me that Ryson could forget himself, forget me, forget us.

Suddenly, I felt sick with the weight of my naivety. Then again, no one had even mentioned that this could happen, so of course, it hadn't crossed my mind.

The doctor went through his normal routine, testing motor skills and touching Ryson's arms and legs and feet, as I fired off text messages to Ryson's mom, Paige, and Madison, letting them know he was awake. Ryson kicked when directed, nodded when he felt pain, and made a fist on command, but he couldn't remember who he was or who I was or almost anything about his life. He had no memory of the accident and swore up and down that he didn't even know how to surf. I stood, staring at the person I loved with all my heart but barely recognized. The things he said, the way he said them—they weren't coming from the person I knew.

I wanted to wretch, and I considered throwing up right there on the sterile white tiles.

"Quinn?" the doctor said my name as he held the door open and gestured for me to go outside with him. We walked out, and he said calmly, "This happens sometimes," as if the words made everything better.

"This happens sometimes?" I repeated his words, feeling angry, upset, and out of control.

Rationally, I knew it wasn't the doctor's fault, but the person I loved more than anything had no idea who I was. I'd never felt so small or insignificant as I did right now.

"I know you're scared. And confused and hurt. But retrograde amnesia from a traumatic brain injury is always a possible side effect."

"What does retrograde mean?"

"It's a type of amnesia. The most common actually. Most patients don't remember the accident or anything before it, although they do usually remember their name and basic information."

"No one ever said anything about it," I said in anger before taking a swift breath and asking, "Is it permanent? Will he get his memory back? What if he never remembers who I am? Or who he is?" I fired off the questions like I was running out of time to ask them even though I knew I wasn't.

"That's always a possibility," the doctor informed me, his tone still annoyingly calm.

How could he be so composed while I was falling apart inside? How could he stay so rational while the last of the threads that held me together were fraying?

"So, it's possible? He might never remember anything?"

"It's possible. But it's not likely, Quinn."

His hand reached my shoulder, and I flinched, moving away from his unwanted touch.

"But it's possible," I repeated, refusing to be mentally caught off guard again. I didn't want to be so blinded by what I hoped would happen and what I wanted to happen that I couldn't see the whole picture. I needed to see it all. If anything was even a remote possibility, it was staying firmly rooted in my mind.

"Like I said, it's possible. But it's not probable. You need to stay positive. Have you called his mother?"

"She's on her way," I said with a nod.

"I'll talk to you both some more once she arrives. Don't worry, Quinn. It will work itself out," he said before tucking his clipboard under his arm and stalking away.

It would work itself out?

Sucking in a steadying breath, I walked back into Ryson's room and pretended to pull it together. He watched me, his brown eyes curious but otherwise emotionless. The love that always reflected in them when he looked at me was nonexistent. I never knew a single look could cause so much heartache.

"Hi," I said, my voice shaky. "Your mom is on her way."

He half-grinned. "I remember her."

"You do?"

"Yeah." He nodded. "My dad coming with her?"

My face instantly changed as I struggled with how to respond. "No. Your dad's not in town." I sounded distressed, and I knew it. "What else do you remember?"

He shrugged. "My parents. Our house. Just like the visual of them, not specific details."

"But you don't remember me?" I didn't want to feel rejected, but I still did. How could I not?

"I'm sorry. I can tell it hurts your feelings that I don't. But I don't know who you are." His voice sounded so cold; it actually sent shivers down my spine.

My eyes squeezed closed to keep the tears from falling. "It's okay. It's not your fault."

"But you're looking at me like you're disappointed."

Even this version of Ryson could read me like a damn book.

"It hurts that you don't remember me. We've been together a long time, and we've been through a lot."

"So, you're what, my girlfriend? Wife?" He sounded suddenly panicked as he looked down at his left hand. When he saw no ring there, I swore, I saw him breathe out in relief.

Jesus. Even this Ryson didn't want to marry me.

"Girlfriend. We're not married or engaged," I said, my tone sounding far more bitter than I had meant it to.

He shifted on his bed, and I could tell that I was making him uncomfortable. I couldn't remember a time when my presence had caused Ryson discomfort instead of peace. Every one of his actions stung, a single blow straight to my chest, quickly followed by another.

Ryson moved again, his dark eyes meeting mine. "I don't mean to be rude, but do you think you could wait outside until my mom gets here?"

"You want me to …" I started to repeat his words back to him as my thoughts tripped over themselves, and I fought back the tears. "Sure. I'll just be outside."

I gathered up my purse and cell phone before walking out his door and pressing my back against the cold wall. *Where was I supposed to go? What was I supposed to do?* I allowed a few frustrated tears to fall as I lowered myself to the floor and buried my head in between my knees. Questions flooded my mind. *What the hell did all this mean for my life if Ryson wasn't a part of it? If he never remembered me, was I just supposed to pretend we never existed? How could I ever walk this earth while he walked it, away from me? That was not how our story was supposed to end—with us apart.*

"Quinn? Why are you sitting out here?" Ryson's mom's voice met my ears.

I had no idea how long I'd been out there. When I looked up at her, her entire expression changed from happiness to worry.

"What's wrong? Quinn, what's the matter?"

She put her hand out for me to grab, and she helped pull me to my feet.

"He doesn't remember me."

A guttural laugh sounded from deep in her chest. "That can't be true."

I sniffed, wiping at my face. "It is. He doesn't know who he is. He doesn't know who I am."

I watched as she inhaled long and hard before reaching for my hand again and squeezing it tight.

"Well, let's go remind him," she said before pushing open his door and walking through it, dragging me close behind.

I DON'T REMEMBER
Ryson

W HEN I'D FIRST opened my eyes, confusion had immediately slammed into me.

Where am I? was the first question that popped into my head, quickly followed by the next ... *WHO am I?* That was the scarier of the two.

I tried and tried in vain to get any answers from my mind, but nothing came. There was nothing there for me to sort through. Aside from a blurry vision of my mom and dad, I had little else to go on.

And then there was the girl. She kept repeating my name over and over again, looking at me like she knew me, but I had no idea who she was. My first thought was that she might be my sister, but for whatever reason, I knew that I had no siblings. I could tell she wanted more from me, far more than I could give, so I had to ask her to leave. She was making me feel worse than I already did, if such a thing were possible.

I knew that my actions and words were hurting her, but how did she think I felt? I had no fucking idea who I was, and no matter how hard I tried to grasp at the information lingering just outside the edges of my brain, it wouldn't let me reach it. It was one of the worst feelings ever—to not remember but be remembered.

The doctors kept telling me that I had gotten hurt in a surfing accident, but I knew damn well that I didn't know how to surf. I'd never even owned a board. No idea how I'd gleaned that information, but I was convinced it was true. They had told me what had happened, but it hadn't felt right.

I trusted my gut, my emotions, since I couldn't seem to trust anything else. If it felt off, I would believe it, and this surfing thing felt off. I had nothing else to work with other than my instincts, so I held on to them with both hands.

The door pushed open, and the woman I knew was my mom stepped through, holding the girl's hand I still couldn't place. She'd claimed she was my girlfriend, but I still felt nothing when I looked at her. There was no flicker of recognition, no spark of knowing, no extra beating of my heart. My mind and heart were blank canvases, and she was nothing but a stranger to me.

I felt powerless, helpless, and pissed off. And all the stares from the doctors, nurses, and my supposed girlfriend didn't help either. It confused me that basic information was available for me to access, like some storage file of useless shit my brain deemed important. I knew the names of objects, like windows and beds, and that I was in a hospital. I could read. I knew what colors were. It was a bunch of pedestrian crap really, if you asked me, because when it came to the important stuff, like remembering actual details of my life, there was nothing there.

The girl looked at me with hurt, sadness, and disappointment in her hazel eyes. A part of me wanted to lie and pretend like I knew who she was for her sake, but most of me just wanted her to go away. *How long had we dated? Did I trust her? Was our relationship good? Did we fight? Did I love her?* So many questions flooded my mind, but none of the answers followed. My brain felt like Swiss cheese, and everything I longed to know had simply slipped away through the holes.

"Hey, sweetheart," my mom said as she rounded the bed and planted a kiss on my head. "I'm so happy you're awake."

"How long have I been asleep?" I asked, realizing that no one had told me that yet.

"A little over a week," she said with a soft smile.

All I wanted to do was go home—not that I remembered what home looked like exactly, but I still wanted to go there.

My mom's smile faded a little as she waved a hand in the girl's direction. "Honey, you don't remember Quinn?"

Quinn.

So, that was her name.

"I don't." I looked at my mom with pleading eyes. I didn't want to do this in front of her. No more questions about her, about us, about the fact that I couldn't remember a damn thing about my life.

"She's been here the whole time, waiting for you to wake up." My mom's voice was smooth, but it stirred up the anger simmering inside of me.

"Isn't that what girlfriends are supposed to do?" I asked

bitterly, my frustration seeping out before I could control it.

"Ryson!" my mom barked.

But I barked back, feeling helpless and out of control, "What? I don't remember her, okay?" I turned toward Quinn and continued my rant, "I'm sorry I don't remember you, but I don't. And you keep making me say it. And every time I do, it hurts you, but you keep asking to hear it. Over and over again. Stop making me hurt you."

Quinn's eyes instantly filled with tears, and even though I knew that I should feel like an asshole for being so blunt, I couldn't bring myself to feel that badly. Everything I'd said was the truth. I was supposed to feel something for her, but I didn't. I was supposed to be kinder, but I couldn't. And I hated myself for it because disappointing people was the worst feeling in the world, even the people you couldn't remember.

"Pull yourself together," my mom snapped at me before reaching for Quinn's shoulder. "Let's go talk outside."

"No," Quinn bit back in response, pulling out of my mom's grasp.

I had to stop myself from laughing. She was as feisty as she was hot. And, yeah, even though I didn't remember her, I couldn't deny that she was drop-dead gorgeous. The only problem was that it didn't change the fact that I still saw a complete stranger whenever I looked at her.

"No?" I gave her a jaded laugh.

"I know you don't remember, but you will."

"You don't know that."

"I do know that."

She took a step toward me, and I suddenly hated that I was lying in this bed, tied to tubes, unable to move. It made me feel even less in control.

Quinn moved closer. "Here. I have pictures that I can show you."

She pulled out her cell phone, and my stomach clenched.

I turned my head away. "I don't want to see them."

"Really?"

"Really."

I met her eyes, and she started to put her phone back into her pocket.

"But it might help." She attempted to sound positive.

"Or it might not." I tried to sound realistic.

"You don't even want to try?"

How could I put this in words that she'd understand?

"It would be like looking at strangers. You want me to remember things I have no memory of. You want me to feel something, but I don't feel anything. I'll look at the pictures and feel even more lost than I do right now."

Tears instantly started spilling down her cheeks even though I could tell she wished they hadn't. She wanted to appear tough, but she was losing the battle.

"Quinn," my mom interrupted, her tone extra calming, like the way she talked to her patients. "I think you should give him some time."

Quinn's eyes darted between mine and my mom's. She looked so damn sad, and I knew it should break my heart, but it didn't. I practically held my breath as I waited for her to agree, and I realized just how desperately I needed her to leave.

Quinn's head nodded slowly as she stared down at her feet. "Okay. I'll go."

Before Quinn could turn to leave, the door flew open, and two guys and two girls walked through it, smiling, laughing, and rushing to my bedside like they hadn't seen me in years. I smiled back at them because they were all so damn happy; I couldn't help myself. They said my name over and over, their giddiness almost contagious enough to make me forget that I didn't know who they were either.

"My man!" One of the guys threw his hand in the air, and I slapped it, knowing to do at least that much in greeting. "We've missed you. How are you feeling? Ready to get out of here or what?"

I opened my mouth to respond, but I wasn't sure exactly what to say.

Quinn spoke up, "He can't leave yet."

"Why not? He looks good," the guy said casually.

Quinn attempted to smile. "He doesn't remember."

"He doesn't remember what?" The guy took a step back, giving me a half-crazed look, his blue eyes pulling together. "Is this a joke? You guys messing with me?" he asked, and I detected a bit of a Southern accent in his voice.

I shrugged my shoulders. "Wish we were."

"What don't you remember?" one of the girls asked as she made her way toward Quinn near the back of the room.

"Anything," I answered.

"You don't know who I am?" Southern-accent guy asked, sounding hurt, and I was so tired of hurting people already.

"Please don't tell me that you're my boyfriend," I said, and the room exploded with laughter.

"Nah, man. Only one person in the world for you, and she's right over there," he said as he pointed toward Quinn, who was the only one not smiling.

"So I've been told."

He cocked his head back, looking completely shocked. "Wait. You don't remember Quinn either?"

My throat felt like it was closing in on me as every pair of eyes in the room drilled into mine. "I don't even remember myself."

He turned to look at Quinn at the same time that the two girls moved to wrap their arms around her as she continued to stare at the ground. She couldn't look at me anymore, I assumed.

"Can I ask you all something?" I announced to the room.

"Of course. Anything."

"Why are you all so good-looking? I feel like I'm watching the cast of a TV show right now."

They all laughed, but it was uncomfortable, and I had no idea what I'd said wrong, but it was clearly something.

"Have you looked at yourself in the mirror? You're just as pretty as we are," the other guy in the room said, his voice strong and commanding.

I actually hadn't looked at myself, to be honest. I had no idea what I looked like, and up until now, it hadn't even occurred to me to check.

"We're all—" he started to say before Quinn stopped

him.

"It doesn't matter," she said as her eyes finally met mine. "If you don't remember, it doesn't matter what we are. We should go."

She turned and walked out of the room. The other two girls quickly followed behind without saying another word to me.

The guys grew conflicted; I could tell. They were shifting their weight and looking from me to the door. They wanted to stay with me but felt obligated to follow the girls out.

"I guess we'll see you later, Ry. Get better." One of them said.

"Sure thing. Thanks for coming." I tried to be polite even though I still felt nothing.

They seemed like good guys, guys I could see myself being friends with, but there was no familiarity there either.

The room grew quiet after they left, and my mom moved into the chair that Quinn used to occupy. "Still nothing?" she asked, and I knew exactly what she meant. *Had seeing that group jogged anything in my memory at all?*

I shook my head. "It's like a totally blank slate. There's just nothing there."

"How frustrating," she said, and at least with her, I felt a little understood.

"I've been friends with them a long time?"

"For the most part. It's a little complicated." She patted my arm, and I wondered what could be so complicated about a group of friends.

"How?"

119

"Huh?"

"How is it complicated?"

Maybe if she said something familiar, my memory would spark or come to life, and all the pieces of this fucked up, broken puzzle would put themselves back together.

I watched as she tried to formulate her thoughts into the right words, the way she always did. It only made me impatient, and I was about to snap at her when she said, "You don't have a normal life, Ryson. You guys aren't just normal kids."

"Mom, please. What does that even mean? Just spit it out already." I shifted in my bed, pulling at one of the pillows behind my back and moving it up higher.

"You're a famous actor."

Her lips pursed together, and I laughed.

"Come on."

"I mean it. Those were your best friends. You're all"— she paused for a breath—"really famous, and you were about to start filming a reality show."

"What the hell is a reality show?"

My mom explained what it meant, and honestly, I thought it sounded stupid as hell and couldn't believe that people watched that kind of crap. But then again, I couldn't picture myself as a famous actor either, so what did I know? Acting felt about as right to me as surfing did.

It didn't.

At all.

Being an actor didn't feel like me, didn't sound like me, and didn't sit right in my guts. And I had no idea why. I mean, if it were true, wouldn't it resonate somehow, tickle the back of my brain, or at least ring with familiarity?

I assumed that it would or at least that it should, but it didn't. It all felt … off.

"Ryson? Did you hear me?" my mom asked.

I refocused my attention back toward her. "I heard you. Reality TV. Sounds awful."

"You were really excited about it."

I felt pressured, pressured to remember, to be exactly the same as I had been before the accident. Everyone wanted me to fit into the mold of who I used to be or who they kept telling me that I was, but I found that nearly impossible.

"Do you know when we can leave?"

My mom uncrossed her legs before standing up. "I'll go find the doctor and ask."

When she left me alone, I pressed my head against the pillow and stared at the tiles on the ceiling, half-wishing I could go back to sleep and never wake up. Turning my head to the left, I spotted a cell phone on the table, plugged into the wall. I knew instinctively that it was mine, but I refused to touch it even though the light on it was flashing incessantly.

It wasn't hard to guess at what I'd find inside if I reached for it. Part of me was curious, but the rest of me wasn't ready. I feared that looking at it would make me resentful for all I'd see and not be able to remember. I didn't want to look at pictures of people who felt like strangers or read messages I knew I wouldn't be able to decipher. My phone felt like a weapon, and its sole purpose was to hurt me.

The door reopened, and my mom came through it, a smile on her face. "Your doctor said if everything goes well through the night and your scans come back normal in the morning, we can leave right after."

"Awesome," I said, feeling a small twinge of freedom shoot through me. It wasn't until that moment that I realized how trapped I felt—in my head, in my emotions, in this world where I apparently had a place but couldn't remember a thing about it.

GOING HOME
Ryson

W HEN I OPENED my eyes the next morning, disappointment flooded my senses. I still had no idea who I was
or any details about my life. At first, all I felt was sadness.
But then it shifted into an anger I hadn't anticipated. I really
wanted to know, wanted to remember, wanted to be normal
again. But that wasn't in the cards. At least, not for today.
Maybe it never would be.

I realized that it had been less than twenty-four hours, but
what if I never remembered? It was a possibility; the doctors
had said so even if they deemed it highly unlikely. Maybe I'd
be in that illustrious small percentile who had to start their
life completely over. Only time would tell.

"Morning." My mom's voice cut a hole through my
thoughts, and I turned to face her.

"Morning."

"Anything new today?" she asked, a hopeful gleam in her
eyes.

I shook my head to salve the defeat. Her expression shifted, the light dimming from her eyes, and I knew she was sad

for me.

"It's okay." She tried to act as if it didn't matter. "The doctor's have all said it would take time."

I pulled myself up, dying to get the hell out of this bed. "But what if my memories never come back?

"Then, we'll deal with it." She leaned forward, gripping my hand in hers. "We'll figure it out."

"Where's Dad? Why isn't he here?" I asked and watched as my mom grew agitated and concerned. "What aren't you telling me?"

She winced slightly, as if weighing what and how much to tell me. "He doesn't live with us anymore."

"What? Since when? You got divorced?"

"Yeah, Ryson, we got divorced."

Nothing made any sense. My parents had been solid. At least, I thought they had been. Maybe I was remembering those details all wrong too.

"Okay, so you got divorced, which I still can't believe," I said, my mind racing. "But where is he? He knows I'm in the hospital, right?"

My mom avoided eye contact with me, and I knew that there was so much more she wasn't telling me. It made me feel worse, knowing that things were being kept from me even if I had no idea what those things were.

"We haven't heard from him in years, honey. I'm sorry."

"Years?" I said through my shock. "I hate this. I hate not remembering anything."

"I can't even imagine how you must feel."

I was grateful for those words because they were true.

She couldn't even begin to imagine how it felt to be me. No one could.

"Not to change the subject, but Quinn's still here."

Every time she said Quinn's name, it was like she expected me to react in a specific way or get some doe-eyed look on my face.

I blew out an annoyed breath. "I thought she said she was leaving."

"She did say that. But she stayed in the waiting room overnight. Just in case you woke up this morning and remembered, she wanted to be here."

I had no idea why, but the fact that Quinn had only moved a few hundred feet away angered me even more. "That girl doesn't know when to quit."

My mom clenched her teeth together in some feeble attempt to keep her emotions in check. She was usually so composed, so pulled together, but I was pushing her—that much I could tell.

"*That girl* is not the type to walk away or give up on you. That's not what she does. And it's not what you do for her in return. Quinn won't just leave you alone because you keep asking her to."

"We'll see," I said with a small shrug.

My mom's face instantly soured. "Son, you have no idea what you and that girl have been through together. And you clearly have no idea how much you love her."

"Exactly!" I practically shouted. "I don't have any idea! None. That's the most realistic thing you've said since I woke up."

"Well, I'm trying to tell you how it was between the two of you. I'm trying to make you see," she said.

Hearing how I was supposed to feel about Quinn didn't make me feel it. Telling me how our relationship used to be didn't make it real.

I cut her off, "I feel like you're telling me a story about someone else's life. You want me to be invested in the story, but I can't connect to it."

"Don't you want to remember?"

"It doesn't matter what I want."

And it didn't because wanting didn't make my memories come back. Longing for a single recollection didn't make one suddenly appear. And trying with all my might to force one free didn't work either. Trust me, I'd been trying.

The door slowly swung open, and Quinn poked her head inside. "I don't mean to intrude. I just wanted to check in and see how you were this morning."

Leveling my mom with a hard glare, I looked back at Quinn and announced, "I still don't remember anything."

"Oh." Her smile faded. "I'm sorry."

She stayed at the door, holding it open with one hand like she was afraid to step all the way inside.

"He's being discharged this morning after they run some final tests," my mom informed Quinn.

I watched the confusion settle in across her face.

"Where's he going to go?" she asked, talking around me like I wasn't even in the room or had a say in the matter. I supposed I didn't.

"I was planning on taking him home," my mom said

before adding, "to my house."

"I see." Quinn swallowed as she stepped completely into the room and let the door fall shut behind her. "He doesn't have any of his things there."

"We'll take the bag that Paige packed." My mom nodded toward a duffel bag sitting on the ground, and I assumed that Paige was one of the girls who had come by last night. "And I can stop by and get more of his stuff later in the week."

"Okay. That's probably for the best," Quinn agreed, her eyes meeting mine.

I could tell that she hoped that I would suggest a different alternative, but I couldn't do that. What was I supposed to say? Where else was I supposed to agree to go?

Quinn eyed my cell phone, which I still hadn't touched, on the makeshift nightstand. "My phone number's in there if you want to talk or text or anything. "Thanks," I said halfheartedly, and we both knew I had no plans on using it.

"I think you have it saved under Honeypot. I know it's not under Quinn." She actually looked embarrassed.

"Honeypot?"

"It was an inside joke." She looked at my mom before looking back at me. "Okay, well, this is awkward." She tried to lighten the mood, but she was right. It was.

"Little bit," I agreed.

"Do you want me to go then?" she asked.

"I think it's for the best. Don't you?"

Quinn ignored my question and moved toward the duffel bag, pulling some of what looked like her things from inside of it. After she zipped it back up, my mom pulled her tight and whispered something I couldn't hear into her ear. Quinn offered a quick nod before walking out of the room without sparing me a single glance.

I felt conflicted by her exit as both relief and guilt pulled at me. Reaching for my cell phone, I searched for Honeypot in the Contact list. Finding it, I changed the name to Quinn before turning it off.

CRUEL REALITY
Quinn

I 'D STUPIDLY STAYED the night in the hospital waiting room, hoping that when Ryson woke up this morning, he'd have his memory back. There was no way in hell that I was leaving, even after he was so cold to me, so indifferent. I knew that he was frustrated, and I tried to put myself in his position, but it was hard. He'd never talked to me the way he had last night, and his words had been difficult to hear.

Paige had texted first thing in the morning to ask me if Ryson's condition had changed. When I'd told her it hadn't but that I was still at the hospital, getting ready to leave, the four of them showed up, ready to support me any way they could.

Once I was out of Ryson's hospital room, I filled them in on what had happened. Madison and Paige each gripped one of my arms as I lost it. They held me, the three of us in some awkwardly positioned hug, as I cried out my frustration and anger and pain onto their shoulders.

"It's going to be okay. He'll get his memory back, and then everything will go back to normal," Paige said, her voice so sweet that I knew she really believed it—or at least, she wanted to.

"What if he doesn't? What if it takes years?" I asked, the shocked realization hitting me like a blunt force.

Days without Ryson would be one thing, but years …

"We won't let it," Madison said, her tone strong.

I let out a guttural laugh because she was insane. "We don't really have control over his amnesia," I argued.

She tsked me and held up a finger. "I'm going to research the hell out of this and look up every single thing they say can help cure it, fix it, shorten it, or whatever. If it exists, I'll find it."

Madison was the fixer. There was no problem too big that she wouldn't at least attempt to tackle. And I loved her for it. Her heart was always in the right place. It was what made her such a damn good agent and friend.

"Last night was awful," Tatum said, his hand rubbing across his jaw. "I mean, it was awful for me to see him like that. I can't imagine how it must be for you." He pulled me into his arms and gave me the tightest hug.

"Having the one person who holds your heart in his hands look at you with zero emotion in his eyes? Pretty fucking brutal," I said as the tears welled again. "I've never felt so small and insignificant before."

"It's like he's a completely different person," Tatum added before we started toward the exit. "He even talks different. It's weird."

"But all the doctors still say it's temporary, right?" Walker asked as we headed near the lobby where a slew of paparazzi waited outside, their hands pressed against the windows as they tried to see in.

I nodded. "They do, but they don't know for sure, you know? They can't make any promises."

"Right. Of course not. But still," Walker said, "it shouldn't last."

"I don't know," I said through my frustration and hurt. "They're still here?" I gave a nod toward the waiting paparazzi. I had noticed them the minute we rounded the corner, cameras in hand, phones stuck to their ears, waiting.

"They came when we did," Madison said through a grimace. "Sorry."

I shrugged. "It's not your fault. And it's not like you can do anything to stop them."

Paige stepped in front of my body to shield me from prying eyes, but it was no use. She was too thin to hide anyone from anything. "Did you want to go home alone? I think I should come with you," Paige offered, and I knew that I needed her. "Tatum can take my car back to our place, or he can follow us to yours. Up to you."

"How many are at the house, do you think?" I asked, referencing the potential amount of press that would be there.

"A lot of them," Madison said.

"A lot of them?" I practically choked.

"Especially once they spread the word that you're leaving the hospital"—she paused—"without Ryson."

My heart started racing. This was one thing I hadn't considered or had time to think about—dealing with the press and their inquisition.

Pulling myself together, I looked at Madison. "What do you think I should do?"

I trusted her opinion, valued it actually, and knew that she had the ability to think more levelheaded than I could ever be in this moment. It wasn't her heart that had been ripped from her chest.

"I think Paige should go home with you," she insisted, looking between me and Paige, who was nodding in agreement.

"I'm not sure sending two girls into the lion's den alone is the smartest idea," Tatum interjected, his jaw flexing. He wasn't a fan of the suggestion, I could tell.

"It's not like we haven't done this before." Paige attempted to calm him down, but Tatum was adamant.

"We have no idea how many people are there. And if you two show up alone, with no security or protection, who says they won't make it impossible for you to drive or get inside the house? What if they try to stop you from closing the gates and they get on the property?"

"And you're going to what, manhandle them?" Paige teased him.

He stood up tall, his chest puffing out. "If I have to." He tossed an arm around Paige and pulled her body against his. "You two are not going alone. I'm going with you. This isn't negotiable."

"It's fine," I said, agreeing with Tatum. "He's probably right anyway. It will be helpful to have him there."

"Why can't we all go?" Walker asked, his deep voice cutting through mine, and I could tell he wanted to be involved, wanted to help, and hated being left out of this.

Madison cleared her throat. "I think we start small. If we all go there like some united front, the press will think we have something to hide. Quinn showing up with just Paige and Tatum won't necessarily ring any alarm bells." She tapped a finger against her lips as her wheels continued to spin. "I need to think about how we're going to handle this going forward. Especially if Ryson doesn't regain his memory anytime soon."

Madison was in full-on work mode. She turned to me. "Sorry."

"Don't be. It's the truth."

"Okay. So, you and Paige should drive together in your car. Tatum, follow behind them. Do not get physical with the paparazzi unless it's absolutely necessary and you can't avoid it." Madison dished out directions to Tatum, and he listened intently. I would have thought it ridiculously sweet and adorable if we had been in some other situation. "They're going to ask you questions, Quinn. Feel free to play it by ear. Stay silent, offer a small smile as you walk into the house, or make a statement. Totally up to you, and I'll handle things on my end, depending on what you choose to do. Sound good?"

This was why Madison was the absolute best, and everyone wanted to be represented by her. She gave me options, choices, and then handled her job accordingly instead of the other way around. Most agents would force you to fit into whatever made their job easier. They hated giving you a choice, wanting you to do things their way and usually insisting upon it. But Madison seemed to instinctively know that I had no idea how I would handle this situation at my front door until I was actually in it. She trusted me to do what felt best, and I was grateful for her level of understanding and compassion.

"Thank you." I pulled her into a hug.

Paige reached for my hand and held it. "Ready?"

"Not really," I admitted but started walking toward the glass exit doors anyway, leaving my heart behind with the guy who no longer wanted it.

WAIT FOR ME
THE PAST
Quinn

"**A**ND THAT'S A wrap, folks," the director yelled from behind her round glasses.

I turned immediately toward Ryson and fell into his open arms. We stood there for longer than was appropriate, holding on to one another like our lives depended on it. I had a feeling that his did.

"We'll get you that help now," I whispered against his neck, and his arms squeezed me tighter in response.

"Come on, you guys. Party's outside," one of our castmates yelled as she exited the stage.

"You ready for this to be over?" He looked at me, his brown eyes now all too familiar, and chills coursed through my body.

I shook my head in response, and he kissed my forehead. I'd never want things with Ryson to be over—not tonight, not tomorrow, not ever. But first things first. He needed to get better; he needed to get clean.

Reaching for my hand, he interlaced his fingers with mine as he pulled me toward the exit. "I don't know what I would have done without you, Quinn. Thank you for not hating me and for not giving up on me."

I smiled. "I care about you, Ryson," I said, and he grinned from ear to ear before I added, "As a friend."

His smile faltered only slightly. "As a friend for now because I still have a problem," he said matter-of-factly. "But once my problem is kicked, so to speak, it's more than friends for you and me, and you know it."

He poked his finger against my chest, and I narrowed my eyes in mock annoyance.

"We'll see. Help first," I said, trying to sound strong when all I wanted to do was shout my agreement and attack his lips with my face. "Then, we'll talk about the rest."

"Yeah, we will. We'll be talking about it with our mouths," he said with a laugh.

"That's how people usually talk, weirdo." I shook my head at him, pushing him to flirt harder.

"I meant, with our mouths and our tongues. We'll be talking with no words, Quinn, because we won't need them."

God, he was arrogant. And it was so damn hot.

"And the next time I go surfing, you'll stay on the sand and wait for me instead of leaving before I'm even out of the water."

"You saw me?" My voice was filled with surprise at being caught.

"I always see you," he said calmly, as if there was no way I could be anywhere near him without his knowledge.

"But you never said anything."

"Neither did you."

Touché.

Ryson and I mingled with the rest of the cast and crew, neither one of us leaving each other's side. I witnessed more than a few hushed whispers aimed in our direction, and I knew that people thought we were together. The fact that Ryson refused to let go of my hand for most of the evening didn't help put out any of those particular fires.

I didn't mind the attention though. The truth was, knowing that I would no longer be seeing Ryson on set every day was more than a little depressing. I'd grown used to hanging out with him and taking care of him. To say I was more than a little attached was a gross understatement. Even my heart slowed down its rhythm in response to our impending separation. It was going to miss him too. I tried giving it a silent pep talk, letting it know that Ryson would be back for us, but I didn't think it believed me.

And later that night, when we finally said our good-byes, I couldn't stop the few tears that had formed from falling. I watched as a single tear spilled from Ryson's eye and felt my heart thump in response.

His thumb gently swiped across my cheek. "I'm coming back for you."

I swallowed hard as I searched for my voice. "I hope so."

"I mean it," he said before pressing his lips against my cheek and then my forehead.

"Will you wait for me?" he asked, and I nodded my response. "Say the words, Quinn. Tell me you'll wait for me. I need to hear it."

His quiet desperation was charming even though it probably shouldn't have been.

"I'll wait for you."

"Promise?"

"Promise," I agreed, not having any idea what I was truly getting myself into.

"I'm going to get better, and then I'm coming for my girl." He pressed a soft kiss to my lips before he turned and walked away.

I tossed up a silent prayer to whoever was listening that his words would be true because I knew deep inside that I would wait.

I'd wait forever for Ryson to come back and get me.

I just hoped it wouldn't take that long.

MALIBU PAPARAZZI

THE PRESENT

Quinn

P AIGE DROVE MY car down Pacific Coast Highway and made the right turn onto the street that would take us to my home. The road was an absolute madhouse, and I was suddenly consumed with embarrassment. I was embarrassed that I'd turned my usually peaceful neighborhood into a circus. And while most of the neighbors never complained about our celebrity status, this might prove to be too much for them to tolerate.

Why were the paparazzi and press allowed to do this kind of stuff—descend on people's homes, invade their personal space, and pretend like they had every right to be there, uninvited?

And why was there literally no protection in place for us—the hounded, the hunted, the pursued?

The phone rang, and I pressed answer on my stereo system.

Tatum's voice reverberated throughout the car. "I was

expecting crazy. I wasn't expecting insanity."

"You and me both, buddy," I agreed, feeling over-whelmed.

There wasn't a single place to park for at least three streets over. Cars, vans, and motorcycles lined every square inch of the neighborhood, and scores of people waited on sidewalks and in the streets with cameras, cell phones, and all kinds of digital equipment. It wasn't just the press either. There were fans as well.

"How do you want to handle this?" Tatum asked as our car slowed to navigate the frenzy as safely as possible.

The constant flashing from cameras was blinding even though it was still light out. Paige honked the horn but never stopped driving. She knew that if we stopped moving altogether, we'd never start back up again.

"I'm going to keep going. They'll either get out of the way or get run over," Paige interrupted with a shrug.

I looked at her with half adoration, half surprise. She was the most understanding of our group, so it was shocking whenever she got mouthy and bossy.

"That's my girl." Tatum laughed before ending the call.

I typed a code into an app on my phone, and the privacy gates swung open. Funny name, considering the fact that they were wrought iron and offered very little in the way of actual privacy. You could still see through them and take pictures, but they stopped visitors from physically getting through. I disabled the alarm system on the house as Paige drove through the open gates, yelling through the window for the press to get out of the way. She waved her arms, asking them to scatter, but they hit the hood of my car instead, their bodies angling to get as close as possible to our faces for the best shot, but we both had on sunglasses.

Good luck trying to read our expressions, assholes, I thought to myself.

"Yeah, good luck," Paige repeated, so maybe I hadn't kept the thought inside after all.

She pulled to a stop in the driveway, and Tatum parked right behind us as the gates closed shut with a bang and a loud clicking sound.

"Let's get inside," Paige said, making a swift move for the driver's door.

But no matter how fast we got in and out of the car, it wasn't quick enough. The questions screamed at our backs, faster than we could avoid them.

"Where's Ryson?"

"Why are you here without him?"

"Is it true that he doesn't remember who he is, Quinn?"

"Is it true he doesn't remember you?"

My steps faltered. I hadn't meant them to, but it was enough of a stumble that if anyone was paying attention—and I knew they all were—they caught it.

That last question. My reaction to it. I'd just given them the answer they craved without saying a word.

Once the three of us were inside the house, I blew out a long breath and doubled over, my hands on my knees. Paige rubbed my back as Tatum headed into the kitchen. I focused on breathing in and out, attempting to calm myself, but the swift interaction with the press had left me rattled.

"It's okay," Paige said as Tatum reappeared, a glass of water in his hand.

"It's not okay. They know. How do they always know everything so quickly?" I said, pulling myself upright and drinking the water in one gulp.

Walking into the kitchen, I put the glass in the sink and leaned against the counter as Paige and Tatum followed close behind.

"I wondered that too. Do they have sources in every place or what?" Tatum asked, his voice thoroughly annoyed.

Paige's expression tightened "It's not about having a source per se. I mean, it's not that hard. They offer money for information. Someone usually bites. I'm so sorry that we couldn't keep this quiet for even a day."

"But you didn't say anything, Quinn," Tatum added, his voice turning hopeful. "You didn't answer their questions, so they still don't know. They're basically guessing until they have confirmation."

I cleared my throat as I looked between them. "I stumbled," I started to explain. "When they asked that particular question about Ryson not remembering me, I stumbled."

"So, we'll say you tripped on a rock. It's fine," Paige answered, trying to reassure me and make me feel better.

I halfheartedly shrugged a shoulder. "They're going to find out eventually, right? We can't keep this kind of secret quiet for long."

"Maybe we won't have to," Paige offered softly. "Maybe he'll wake up tomorrow and remember everything."

"That would be nice, wouldn't it?" I asked as my facade fell apart, and emotions swept through me. I sensed in my gut that Ryson wouldn't wake up tomorrow and remember who he was, who I was, or who we were, no matter how badly I wished he would.

"Tell me what we can do to help," Tatum said, shifting on his feet.

Men hated feeling powerless, and I knew this situation was no different.

"Stay here tonight? If that's okay," I said, not wanting to be alone with the press outside and no one else inside. I knew I'd feel trapped and isolated and deathly alone. I wasn't ready.

Tomorrow, I promised myself. Tomorrow, I'd be better.

"Of course we will," Paige said as she looked between her boyfriend and me. "Right, babe?"

"You know I love that guest room." He gave me a wink, and I actually laughed as I pictured it.

Paige always stayed in our girliest room, appropriately named The Goddess Quarters, and seeing Tatum surrounded by a silver-and-blue Disney-themed room was one of the most ridiculous sights ever. But totally worth it.

"One question." Paige cocked her head to the side, and I gave her a slight nod to continue. "We baking tonight?"

Paige knew that I liked to bake away my feelings, but the thought hadn't even crossed my mind. Not once since Ryson's accident had I wanted to try a new recipe, bake a cookie, or frost a cupcake.

"Not this time," I said and watched the realization dawn across Paige's face.

This was beyond fixing.

I was beyond fixing.

HOUSE IS TOO BIG
Quinn

I HAD LITTLE recollection of what we'd done all day to pass the time. Paige and Tatum never left my side, and when I tried to turn on the television, mostly out of habit, Paige stopped me. She refused to let me search the internet either, saying that I wouldn't like what I found there right now. Instead of arguing, I listened to her, knowing full well that she had my best interests at heart.

I remembered sitting outside, the three of us soaking up the sun as I cursed the thing for missing the memo that my world was supposed to be dark now. She refused to stop shining. And I hated her for it. It was funny how the things that had brought you joy in the past, like sunshine, could suddenly feel like the enemy.

Tatum eventually barbequed and tried to feed us. I had a snippet in my head of playing with my food instead of actually eating it. And when my parents called, wanting to come over, I told them that I wasn't feeling up for it but asked them to please get my childhood room ready. I had a vague notion that staying here would at some point become unbearable, and I'd need to leave. Sometimes, when life got too rough, you needed your mom and dad for comfort. I supposed that was what Ryson was doing too.

As night fell, I told Paige and Tatum good night and walked through my bedroom door, stopping mid-step when I caught sight of the bed. My feet refused to move, and my breath started to catch. Ryson had always held on to me so tight when we slept together, claiming that holding me helped him sleep through the night. This was *our* bed. *What was it now? Was it just mine? Would Ryson ever sleep in it with me again? Would he ever remember that this was his home and that I was his girl?*

Lowering my body to the hardwood floor, I crossed my legs and stared at the California king. *Could I sleep there without him? Should I try to sleep in the other guest room instead?* Everyday tasks seemed harder than usual as I second-guessed, questioned, and wondered if there would be a consequence for each decision I made from here on out.

If I slept in our bed, was I somehow telling the universe that I was fine without him and didn't need him by my side? Would it continue to keep him from me because of it? Was this all some kind of test?

Driving myself crazy, I shook my head to chase the thoughts away as I changed into my pajamas and slipped into my side of the bed. It felt too big, too cold, and too empty. I sat alone in the darkness with nothing, except the whirring sound of the fan and my breathing. And I waited for sleep to find me. But it never did.

Before tonight, I'd never understood how people couldn't

fall asleep. It was such a foreign concept to me, the girl who could sleep twelve hours a night if she was allowed. I always assumed that you would eventually grow tired and your body would demand to shut down. But I was wrong.

Whenever I had been stressed out or worried in the past, I always found myself *extra* tired, not less. But this was different. This was loss, an extension of grief. And, apparently, grief kept you wide awake. It forced your mind to race, your head to fill with thoughts, and your memories to replay in ways that didn't allow for sleep. Nothing was allowed to interrupt grief's assault on your senses. It completely fucked you over.

Ryson had checked into rehab immediately after we wrapped, which I learned through my manager, who relentlessly badgered me with questions about Ryson's behavior on set. He was looking for something juicy that he could sell to the tabloids, I could tell.

My insides sparked to life with their desire to protect Ryson, to fight for him, to not let the public tear him down in his absence. I informed my nosy manager that Ryson had been nothing but professional on set and that I hoped he got better. Then, I told him to stop looking for trouble where there wasn't any, and he laughed, clearly mocking me. I wanted to punch him through the phone. I fired him instead. Sucking in a breath as I ended the call, I thought about Ryson and sent him good energy, hoping he was getting better.

My mom told me not to get my hopes up when it came to

him, but I knew she was only trying to protect me. The last thing a parent wanted was their only daughter dating a drug-addicted actor. But knowing Ryson had actually voluntarily checked into rehab, just like he'd promised me he would, I was hopeful. He was proving to be a man of his word.

Grabbing a notebook and a pen, I opened up my laptop and searched the internet for everything I could find about overcoming addiction. I took notes on what was expected from a patient and frowned to myself when I read about how they should stay out of relationships for at least a year, if not longer.

Apparently, most facilities emphasized creating a new relationship with yourself before trying to have one with someone else. They stressed the importance of loving who you were as a person, respecting a higher power, and having a good sponsor. I jotted down things as quickly as I could read them, stopping a couple of times to print full articles and highlighting the parts that seemed relevant.

I wanted to be prepared, if that was even possible. Even if the smallest part of me questioned Ryson's intentions, the rest of me trusted that he would come for me when he was able. And I planned on being ready. Well, as ready as a girl could be when it came to Ryson Miller.

The memory faded as I glanced over at the clock. It was still way too early—or late, depending on how you looked at it—and I groaned to myself as I pushed out of bed. If I wasn't going to get any peace or sleep, I wanted out of this damn room. It held too many memories, and I had too many unanswered questions floating in my head.

Walking down the hallway and into the kitchen, I never realized how big this stupid house was. It had never felt too big before, but now, it felt overwhelming. Like I could disappear and get lost inside of it and never be found if I wanted. When I'd been alone in the past, when Ryson was away filming, it'd never once felt like something that could swallow me whole.

I knew it only felt that way now because I wasn't sure that Ryson would come back this time. And I knew I'd never step foot in here again if that happened—that finality. I remembered that we had both fallen in love with this place the minute we walked through it, but what had sealed the deal was the backyard. With views of the Pacific Ocean and our own private pool, we had taken one step outside, and at the same time, we'd both declared that we wanted it.

I remembered laughing.

I remembered being happy.

I remembered thinking this was the start of our forever as he'd held me in his arms and kissed me.

And now, what was it? There was no way in hell that I could live here without him. I'd burn it all to the ground first.

The sound of soft footsteps startled me, and I looked over my shoulder to see Paige yawning and stretching as she made her way toward me.

"Why are you up so early?" I asked, placing a teapot on the stove and waiting for the water to heat.

"I heard you get up. I didn't want you to be alone."

"You didn't have to do that." I pretended to encourage

her to go back to sleep, but to be honest, it was nice to have her awake with me.

"I know I didn't have to, Quinn. I wanted to. You're my best friend. You've been there for me above and beyond before. Let me be here for you," she offered, and I nodded in silent acceptance.

I had been there for Paige when she ran away, fought with her agent, broke up with her shitty ex-boyfriend after being humiliated, and met Tatum. But it never felt like something I was required to do or did in the hopes that, one day, it would be repaid. It was simply what friends did for one another. I just wasn't used to being on the receiving end, honestly. Ryson and I had been solid for years. There was very little drama in our lives. My friends hadn't had to *be there* for me.

"Have you heard from him at all?" she asked as she pulled out a chair and sat down, running her fingers through her short brown hair.

I shook my head. "No."

Her face pinched, her pain for me apparent. "What are you going to do? I mean, will you text him? Call him? Go see him? We could all go visit him together."

The kettle started to whistle, and I moved to grab two mugs from the cabinet, assuming that Paige would want some too. Seeing Ryson's favorite *Whiskey makes me frisky* mug made me pause. Reaching around it, I pulled out two of my hand-painted Malibu cups before looking at Paige. "I'm going to combine green tea and ginger. It's weird, but I like it. Do you want some?"

"Yes. I like weird." She gave me a half-smile.

Opening up the teabags, I placed them inside the mugs before pouring the steaming water. I grabbed a jar of local honey and a couple of spoons before sitting down across from Paige. It was too early to go in the backyard; the ocean air made it way too cold this time of morning.

"His mom said that she'd keep me in the loop. He was upset yesterday that I was still at the hospital. He *wanted* me to leave."

She glanced down before meeting my eyes again. "I can't even imagine that. I'm so sorry. This has to be so awful for you."

"It is," I agreed as I spooned some honey into my cup and gently stirred it. "And I feel guilty."

"Guilty? Why on earth do you feel guilty?"

"We were fighting. And I keep thinking over and over again in my head that if we hadn't been, maybe he wouldn't have gone surfing in the first place, and none of this would be happening right now."

"It's not your fault." She blew at her tea before taking a tentative sip. "What were you guys even fighting about? You never fight," she asked before listening as I filled her in on our stupid argument and all the things we'd said to one another. It wasn't the first time we'd argued about the idea of marriage, and Paige knew it was the single sticking point in our relationship, so she wasn't necessarily surprised.

"Tatum didn't tell you?"

Her face twisted. "How would Tatum know?"

I offered up a quick shrug. "He was here that afternoon. I

thought maybe Ryson had talked to him about it before he left, but I'm not sure."

"You know how guys are," she started. "They don't really sit around and talk about their feelings."

A small smile played at my lips. "You're right," I agreed. "It's all so unimportant now anyway."

"What is?"

"I just mean"—I took a sip of my drink—"who cares about marriage if your boyfriend can't even remember who you are? I couldn't give two shits about getting married, being married, the piece of paper, or the last name. I just want him back. I just want him to remember me again." My eyes began to water, and I felt myself getting more emotional than I had anticipated.

"I'd want the same thing," Paige said softly as she reached across the table and placed her hand on top of mine.

"I know you would. I wish I could rewind the clock and take it all back."

"I can't believe this is even happening, to be honest. It's like something straight out of a movie. And trust me, I see the irony in that."

I found myself nodding. I'd thought the same exact thing before—how this read like a movie script or a best-selling book. "You should have seen the way he looked at me," I added, giving the proverbial knife in my chest a little twist. "There was no emotion there. No feelings. No compassion. I never realized how much that man loved me with his eyes until he stopped."

"You're breaking my heart." Paige wiped away a tear of

her own, the sadness reflected in her body language and expression. "Maybe today will be different. Maybe he'll remember everything when he wakes up." She sat up straight and tried to be reasonable, but I wasn't in a reasonable state of mind.

"Maybe," I said, not truly believing it would happen.

"You have to be positive," Paige chastised me, as if my state of mind could alter Ryson's.

"I *want* to be positive. But I *need* to be realistic."

"Be positively realistic then." She tried to find middle ground, and I grinned.

"Fine." I settled. "I positively realize that today might be the day where he remembers it all." She smiled, and I added, "Or it might not be."

Her smile dropped as she stared at me. I had no idea what was going on in that head of hers.

"Quinn Lagatha Johnson," she said, playing the game where we made up middle names for each other and randomly used them in conversation.

"Lagatha?" I asked as a small giggle escaped. It felt good to laugh.

"Yes. Quinn Lagatha Johnson," she repeated. "How the heck are we supposed to navigate this? Are we all supposed to sit by and do nothing while we just wait for him to come back to us?"

And in that moment, when she said the word *us*, I realized that I wasn't the only one who'd lost Ryson. We all had. This accident hadn't only affected me. It altered our entire group, changed our dynamic, and broke everyone's heart in almost equal measure.

"I guess we just take it one day at a time. What else can we really do?"

"What are you girls gabbing about this early?" Tatum's deep voice filled the air as he stepped into the kitchen.

How we hadn't heard his manly feet stomping toward us, I had no idea.

Paige stood from her chair and kissed him good morning. Envy surged, but I shoved it back down where it belonged.

"Morning, babe," he said as he wrapped Paige in his arms before looking at me. "Morning, other babe."

He grinned, and unable to resist his charms, I found myself grinning back.

"Did we wake you?" I asked, feeling a little bad.

"Yeah, but I don't mind as long as you feed me coffee." He looked around, his eyes searching for a machine.

"I'll get you some," I said before heading toward the fancy contraption, determined to succeed.

Every time I'd tried to be sweet and make one for Ryson, he always had to come in and save the day. Since I didn't drink the stuff, I never figured out how to use it right. In my defense, the coffeemaker wasn't a simple machine. It was a monstrosity that Ryson had insisted was the best—something about the way it ground the beans just right.

Pressing buttons and opening parts before closing them again, I realized I had zero idea what the hell I was doing. I turned back toward Tatum. "I'm sorry. I honestly have no idea how this thing works. Maybe you speak its language?"

Tatum laughed and walked toward me. "I definitely

speak coffee. I got this. Go sit," he insisted, and I willingly obliged.

My phone pinged, and I practically jumped, the sound surprising me. I'd turned on the Do Not Disturb feature, which meant that only a few select people could get through if they tried to reach me. My heart leaped at the thought that it might be Ryson telling me that he remembered and that he loved me and that he was wondering where the hell I was.

Reaching for it, I saw Madison's name instead.

"Who is it?" Paige's face lit up, her expectations clearly the same as mine, before I turned the screen toward her, so she could read it herself. "Oh," she said, sounding as disappointed as I felt.

Pressing the button to display the message, I read it out loud, "*Ryson left the hospital late yesterday afternoon after getting the all-clear from his doctors. It was an absolute madhouse. My phone has been ringing off the hook for interviews. The press knows that Ryson went to his mom's instead of coming home with you, and they're going nuts over it. I have a call with his mother later this afternoon. I thought you would want to know.*"

"I'm sorry, Quinn." Paige made a sad face as the coffee machine suddenly whirred to life, making noises that sounded like it was actually working properly.

I turned toward Tatum. "You do speak coffee."

"Told you. And hey"—his voice was deep, that Southern accent still strong—"he's going to remember, okay? Maybe not today. Or tomorrow. But, eventually, he'll come back to us." He said it with such determination that I wondered who he was trying to convince more—himself or me.

"I know you've lost your best friend too."

"My guy best friend," Tatum clarified before looking at Paige. "But, yeah, I can't imagine being in this town without him. It's not right."

"Tell me about it," I agreed before typing out a response to Madison, thanking her for the update.

If this was the way things were going to be from here on out—getting information about my boyfriend from a secondhand source—I would have a lot of hard times ahead of me.

I LIVED LIKE THIS?
Ryson

APPARENTLY, IT WAS standard procedure to leave a hospital via wheelchair after a situation like mine. Even though I complained, I wasn't legally allowed to walk off the premises on my own two feet, and no one prepared me for the onslaught that waited outside.

Even though I'd pushed everyone who claimed to be a part of my old life out of it and refused to check my phone, I still felt resentful. A little heads-up from someone other than my mom, who'd clearly had no idea the level of insanity that waited for us outside, might have been helpful. As it was, we found ourselves completely unprepared and overwhelmed.

Flashes went off in every direction as the sound of camera shutters clicking filled the air. The sheer amount of people surrounding us was no match for the hospital security guards who tried to help us navigate our way to the car. My name was being screamed in every direction, more than seemed possible. Questions, comments, and people begging for pictures competed with all the other noise. And when my mom finally stopped the damn wheelchair so I could get the hell out of it and walk on my own, a group of teenage girls started hysterically crying and hugging each other like they'd just witnessed a miracle.

How had I lived this way in the past? It was fucking awful. I felt like a zoo animal on display, everyone ogling, pointing, and taking pictures of me to show their friends.

One of Quinn's girlfriends suddenly appeared out of thin air and reached for my arm, "Why haven't you answered my texts?"

"I haven't checked my phone," I said, annoyed.

I tried to move out of her grip, but she was tougher than she looked, her blonde hair swishing around in a tight ponytail as she gave me a look that would make most men wince.

"I could have helped with your release," she hissed toward me. "Gotten you a police escort and taken care of the press. You have to let me help you, Ryson."

As I fought to remember who she even was, she started addressing the crowd like she owned it, "Everyone, please back up and give Ryson space. He won't be speaking to the press today, but we will have a statement for you soon. As you can see"—she waved a hand in my direction—"Ryson has been released from the hospital and will be recovering from his injuries at home with his mother."

Someone cut her off and shouted, "Why isn't he going home with Quinn? Where is Quinn?"

That started a thousand questions about my supposed girlfriend, where she was, and why the hell I was going anywhere without her.

"Like I said, we'll have a statement for you soon. Until then, please give Ryson, his family, and Quinn some privacy." She looked around and seemed to take stock of every single person in attendance. "I know who you all are. If any of you harass them, I'll find out about it, and we won't work with you again." She pointed a finger at them. "Understood?"

Damn.

This chick was hard-core. Even though she seemed way too young to have garnered that much respect from the crowd of mostly grown men, they all seemed to obey her orders.

"That's all for now. You each have my contact information should you need anything further. Please reach out to me directly for inquiries or interview requests."

She stepped away, to signal the end of the mock press conference, as the shouting and screams continued being hurled. "Let's go," she demanded, and I felt like I should listen.

"Who are you exactly?"

Her head cocked to the side as she groaned, "Your agent." She stopped in front of a blacked-out Audi. "Now, get in the car."

My mom thanked her and gave her a hug as I loaded myself into the unfamiliar passenger seat.

"Paparazzi are going to follow you home. You know that, right?"

My mom nodded toward my agent before sparing me a quick glance. "We have security cameras around the property, and I'll park in the garage. But we don't have a privacy gate or anything like that to keep them out." She sounded nervous, and it made me uncomfortable.

"It's okay," my agent reassured her. "They can't be on your property, but there's no law against them standing on the sidewalk or the street. Close your blinds. Don't give them window access with those ridiculous zoom lens cameras they have. If you give them a way to see inside the house, they'll do it. So don't give them a way."

"What do I do?" I asked, hating the way everyone seemed to talk around me instead of to me. This was my life, and I wanted to be included in the conversation about it.

"Nothing. Please don't talk to anyone until we figure out how we're going to handle this. And maybe pray that you wake up tomorrow and remember who you are, so we can put this all behind us." She smiled sweetly as she turned to leave before stopping and facing me again. "Oh, and, Ryson? I need you to check your messages from me, please. I work for you, but I can't do that if you're not talking to me."

"Fine," I said. "But you're going to need to remind me what your name is. That would probably help in the whole *checking messages from you* front," I said.

"First of all, New Ryson has an attitude problem," she said, clearly unamused. "Second, my name is Madison Myers. Try not to forget it."

"You're hilarious," I said, trying to sound bored.

MADISON HAD BEEN right about the paparazzi staking out our

family home. They had arrived before we did and were waiting for us as we pulled down the street. Bodies and camera lenses crashed into the side of the car and the window.

"I'm sorry, Ryson. I don't want to run anyone over," my mom said as she slowed the car down to a ridiculous pace.

"Just get us inside, please." I knew I sounded like a baby, but I hated this—being in a fishbowl, unable to escape or get away, and not remembering why this was all happening in the first place or how to go about navigating it. "Is it always like this? I mean, for you when you drive home?"

She laughed, and I realized it was the first time I'd heard my mom laugh since I woke up.

"God, no! It's only like this if you and Quinn come over, but I usually go to your house instead. It's much prettier," she said before snapping her mouth closed, as if she'd said something she shouldn't have.

"Where is it? Quinn's house?"

"It's not just Quinn's house. It's your house too. And it's in Malibu," she said.

I shook my head. Again, it was something else that felt off and wrong.

"Why are you shaking your head at me?" She pressed a button on her visor, and a garage door rolled open up ahead.

"Because nothing feels right. The acting, surfing, the beach, Malibu ..." I exhaled loudly. "I don't even like the ocean!"

My mom glanced at me with sadness before turning onto a driveway and pulling straight into the open garage. When she turned off the ignition, the garage door closed behind us as she faced me. "You love the ocean. Or at least, you used to. And you really love surfing. It saved your life once."

"And it almost took it once, too, apparently."

"I can't imagine how hard this is for you. To not remember anything. To have the things you do hear not make any sense. I'm really sorry you don't remember."

She offered me a solemn smile before opening the driver's door and getting out of the car. And without any warning, I was sorry I couldn't remember too.

PLAN OF ATTACK
SEVEN DAYS LATER
Quinn

O NE UNIMAGINABLE DAY had eventually turned into seven of them, each one worse than the one before. A whole week without Ryson. One-hundred and sixty-eight hours of no contact and ignored text messages. Not that I had been counting or anything.

I had totally been counting.

Three. That was the number of text messages I'd sent to Ryson over the past week.

A tiny number, I'd convinced myself. A blip really when compared to the amount of texts we used to send to each other daily. Only three messages in seven days—child's play.

Three. The same number of texts that he had read but didn't respond to.

Being ignored hurt. It hurt so damn bad.

His mom had started texting me each morning—an update on his mental status, I considered it. It was a hellish text to read—that he remembered nothing—but I'd come to expect it. It was how I started my days now—with the confirmation that I continued to mean nothing to the one person who still meant everything to me.

I realized how surprised I'd actually feel if his mom eventually texted me otherwise because no amount of wishing, bartering with God, or hoping had altered Ryson's state of mind thus far. And even though the doctors were convinced that his amnesia wouldn't last, it sure as hell didn't feel that way.

Eventually, I'd gone to my parents' house to get away. The second I left, I felt incomplete and hollow. I went stir-crazy at my mom and dad's, desperate to leave the house and bedroom that no longer felt like where I belonged; it hadn't for years.

So, I quickly came back home to Malibu. I thought I'd hated being here, in our shared home, but I'd hated being away from it just as much. But once I returned, I was desperate to get away again, the ghosts of my lost love haunting me in every corner. Peace and solace eluded me. I longed for a distraction, but nothing helped. I realized pretty early on that I couldn't outrun my mind ... or my broken heart. Whether I was home, checking my emails, driving in the car, or at the grocery store, my grief was a part of me, and I wore it like a jacket.

With Ryson's condition still unchanged, the press grew more invasive and impatient. They wanted answers. They demanded interviews. The more I tried to avoid them, the more lies they printed. Since I gave them nothing to go on, they felt forced to make things up.

They started reporting that Ryson had dumped me, which was fueled further by the fact that he wasn't currently recovering in our shared home. It was kind of hard to dispel any breakup rumors when we were no longer being seen together and both of us had stopped posting on our social media accounts.

I couldn't win, and I knew it. There was nothing I could do that wouldn't be misconstrued or taken out of context. If the press caught me smiling—like the one time I'd gotten caught grinning slightly over something Paige had said—they would report on how happy I was and how over Ryson I seemed to be. I apparently had a new man in my life and had cheated on Ryson before the accident even happened.

If they saw me looking sad, they would print my devastation, splashing my pained expression on every media source they could find. They'd reported that I was suicidal, on a twenty-four-hour psychiatric watch, and couldn't be left alone. Whatever they deemed fit to print, they printed with no regard for who it hurt or affected.

All I wanted was the tiniest sense of normalcy. To do one single thing the way I used to when Ryson was by my side.

I went to the grocery store in hopes that I could grab a few things I needed and not be harassed, but even that was too much to ask. I should have known better. Actually, I did know better, but I went anyway.

The lies had only grown, the headlines screaming at me from the checkout aisle.

Quinn & Ryson Over!
Ryson Dumps Quinn for Cocaine!

Accident a Cover-Up for Rehab!
Ryson Using Again. Almost Died This Time!
Quinn Kicks Ryson Out of Shared Malibu Home
"It's me or the drugs."—Quinn's Ultimatum

My anger soared to another level, and I grabbed the hideous papers, throwing every one of them down on the conveyer belt in a crumpled mess. The cashier stared at me, her eyes wide and shocked as I continued pulling them off the racks like a lunatic.

"Ring them up. I'll buy them all," I thought I shouted. I wasn't sure.

I noticed the cell phones pointed in my direction, filming my emotion-filled rampage, but I didn't care. They were calling Ryson a drug addict again, and I refused to stand by and let people read that trash. The cashier actually looked scared of me as she handed me my receipt. And as soon as I stepped outside, I was bombarded by bodies, my arms overflowing with the printed paper lies. Maneuvering around the cameras and doing my best to ignore their shouts, I tossed the stacks into the trunk of my car before getting in and driving home. I had given them exactly what they wanted—a reaction, something to film, something new to sell.

My stomach turned at the sight of more paparazzi lying in wait to disrupt my privacy. They'd been camped outside my house ever since I came back from the hospital with Paige. They were also stationed out front of Ryson's mom's house, my parents' house, Paige's place, and Walker's home. Anything for a story or a sound bite worth twisting for their agenda.

Sometimes, it felt like the paparazzi were the worst kind of people. I knew that they had a job to do, but why hadn't anyone ever stopped to think about why this type of around-the-clock harassment was considered a job in the first place? There needed to be laws or at least some kind of restrictions in place.

If they stopped reporting on celebrities twenty-four/seven, the public would eventually stop wanting to know every single detail about their lives. When people didn't know that they were missing anything in the first place, they stopped asking for more. But as long as the press posed questions and attention-grabbing headlines that demanded to be read at all hours of the day and night, the public's need was insatiable.

It was a vicious cycle.

One I found that I hated being a part of, especially after my grocery store rampage, which immediately started trending online.

That was why I didn't leave the house for the next day and a half. I couldn't bear to go outside and face the cameras anymore. I stopped putting myself in the position where they could take a picture of me and twist it any way they wanted.

It was exhausting.

The lies ate away at me.

My heart broke all over again with each mention of Ryson's name. Even though people didn't know exactly what, they all knew that something bad had happened between us. Even I wasn't a good enough actress to keep that fact hidden.

Three swift raps on my front door drew my attention before the knob turned, and Madison and Walker stepped through.

"Hello?" Madison yelled, closing the door behind her, the sound of paparazzi fading into nothing as the door latched shut.

"In the kitchen," I shouted back.

"Hey. How are you?" Madison asked with a hug, and I practically fell into her arms.

"Hanging in there, I guess."

"No more grocery store visits?" Walker asked, light-hearted and only meant to tease, but I wasn't in the joking mood.

"I haven't left the house since."

"We know," Madison said.

Even though I'd been ignoring her calls and texts, of course she knew. She always seemed to know everything about her clients.

The front door swung open again, and my eyes grew wide with nerves.

"Paige?" Madison yelled, and Paige answered back.

They'd all come by at the same time, unannounced.

"Is this an intervention?" I asked, feeling suddenly ganged up on instead of whatever this was supposed to be.

"Of sorts," Madison answered as Paige and Tatum appeared in the kitchen, both wearing solemn smiles.

"Don't treat me like I'm going to break. Tell me why you're all here," I said before my heart dropped. "Did something happen to Ryson?"

"No, no. He's fine," Madison quickly said, feeling bad. "Didn't mean to scare you."

I breathed out, leaning against the counter. "Then, what's going on?"

"We all came here, so we could come up with a plan of attack," Paige said, wiggling her eyebrows like the idea excited her.

"A plan of attack?" I asked, confused. "Who are we attacking?"

"The press!" Walker grinned.

"Yeah. We need to do something," Paige added.

"Wait." I held up a hand. "We're attacking the press? I don't understand."

"Don't you hate all the lies?" Walker asked.

I immediately thought that I could ask him the same thing. The press used to scandalize him daily and nightly before he and Madison were a couple. If you believed all the things that they'd printed, you would think that Walker was the biggest asshole on the planet.

"I don't particularly enjoy them," I admitted. "They make me want to throw up, especially when they print something about him. My stomach lurches whenever I read it. And I want to scream at the top of my lungs about how it's total bullshit. How can anyone just believe the things they read?"

"They don't know any better, Quinn." Tatum's voice sounded smooth as we all focused our attention on him. "The public believes these things because they don't have any other knowledge to counter it with. Back in my hometown, if I'd read this stuff online, I would have believed it too. I wouldn't have known otherwise."

I realized how easy it was for me to forget that there was a whole other world outside of Los Angeles. A world where people weren't raised on the entertainment industry and the nuances that being in it involved.

Paige was nodding her head along with her boyfriend's assessment. "It's true. They have these made-up notions of what they think our life is like, so none of these things sound that far-fetched. Plus, you know how obsessed they are with you and Ryson. They'll read anything they can when it comes to the two of you."

"So, we think you should talk to them," Walker clarified before adding, "Things have gotten out of hand."

"I obviously agree," I said, referring to my grocery store fiasco.

"You don't have to do it alone though, if you don't want. We could schedule an interview with all five of us together, but we need to say something."

"Are you my agent now?" I asked a little too sarcastically.

"No. But my girlfriend is," Walker responded in kind.

Madison jumped in. "Remember when they were spreading lies about Paige, and we told her that she needed to stand up for herself and tell her side of the story?"

I nodded because, of course, I remembered. This felt a little different than what had happened with Paige though. To be honest, maybe it only felt that way because it was happening to me.

"It's not going to stop. Ignoring it won't make it go

away."

"You're right." I closed my eyes for a second. "But the only way to get them to stop is to tell them the truth," I practically whispered.

"And?" Madison dragged out the word, understanding that I was hesitating.

"And once I say it out loud, I can't take it back. My story stops being just mine. It becomes everyone's as well."

It had been one thing to share Ryson with the public while we were still together and a couple, but sharing this version of him, the version that didn't remember or even want to be with me, was going to hurt like hell.

Madison nodded as understanding dawned. "You're absolutely right. It does."

"The fans have always felt like Ryson belonged to them. But he belongs to me, you know? They feel like they own part of him, but he's always been all mine. Or at least, he used to be." It pained me to imagine the things people would say.

Paige started talking, "You need to say something anyway. If you don't, then all these people who are making claims, spreading lies about Ryson and you"—she sucked in a quick breath, no doubt remembering the personal hell she'd gone through with the tabloids—"well, they'll win. No one is standing up for him. He can't do it himself right now. If that was me who had amnesia and everyone on the face of the planet was saying that I was back on drugs, that I beat you and broke up with you, then I'd want you guys to say something. I'd want you to set the record straight. I'd want someone to defend my honor because I couldn't do it."

"They're saying he beat me?" I asked, feeling horrified. That was one headline that I'd clearly missed.

"It's been online in a couple of places, yeah," Walker said solemnly.

"I think we should schedule a few print interviews and at least one on camera," Madison said, bringing us back on point. "We can choose who we want to work with. Someone we trust to not sensationalize it."

I hopped up on the counter and exhaled. "Don't you think I should talk to Ryson about all this first?"

"Are you talking to him now?" everyone basically asked, their words overlapping each other.

"No. I talk to his mom. He doesn't answer any of my texts, so I've stopped sending them."

"Does he at least read them?" Paige asked, realizing that I hadn't share this information with her.

I nodded. "Yeah. But there's never any dancing dots, so he doesn't even consider responding back. It's like the ultimate rejection every time."

"He probably doesn't know what to say to you," Madison offered.

I realized in that moment that she had either talked to or seen him. I could sense it.

"You've seen him," I said. It wasn't a question.

Shaking her head quickly, she countered, "No. No. But I talked to him on the phone yesterday."

Must be nice, I thought to myself as bitterness and jealousy raced through me.

"What did he say?" I hated this. Absolutely fucking hated having to ask someone else about my boyfriend. The fact that Madison knew things about him that I didn't stung like a thousand bee stings.

"He just seems really lost. He wavers between being sad about it all and then being really pissed off about it all," she said, and I found myself laughing a little because it sounded just like him. "It's hard to talk to him from a business standpoint because he has absolutely zero recognition of who he used to be. And that frustrates him. He's hung up on me. Twice."

"I want to see him," I said, hopping down from the counter. "Someone take me to see him."

"Right now?" Paige asked.

"Yes, right now. We need to talk to him about all of this. Give him a chance to have an opinion," I said, still wanting to include my teammate in our decision-making process. "Now, which one of you is driving?"

THE GANG'S ALL HERE
Ryson

MY PHONE NEVER stopped ringing, so I turned it off. My agent was going to be pissed, but I couldn't care less. What the hell did I need an agent for anyway? I had no plans on acting again, not as long as I was this version of myself.

The voice mail on my phone was full, and it was a good thing that I didn't have to enter a password anymore to hear them; otherwise, all those voice mails would have stayed unheard. My Mom had unlocked my phone one night when I couldn't get into it. I had been sitting in my room, trying to think of what the hell my password might even be, but nothing came to mind. Nothing ever fucking came to mind. The emptiest of slates, the blankest of canvases—that was what my mind currently consisted of. I listened to the sheer amount of interview requests, knowing I wouldn't call any of them back. What the hell was I supposed to say? They all wanted to talk to someone I couldn't remember anything about.

My mom informed me that no one had publicly confirmed my amnesia yet, so it was still this ridiculous secret everyone was keeping. She also let me know that once it did come out, I could expect the requests to triple. It made me want to throw away my phone. Or at least get a new one.

My head ached. My head always seemed to ache these days. Doctors said it was a side effect of the trauma and should go away with time. But they also said that I'd get my memories back too. And so far, both were lies.

"Your head still hurting?" my mom asked as she entered the living room, which had become my new favorite place to be. I lived on this couch, remote in hand, baseball on the TV.

"Yeah."

"Do you want to go through any pictures today?" She encouraged me with a smile.

I wasn't sure if it was the psychiatrist in her or just her nature in general, but she'd been asking me this every day since we came back.

So far, I'd agreed to it once, but it'd ended in such disaster that I refused to put her through that again. I had a breakdown as we looked at old family photos and got to pictures that included my dad. I couldn't remember when he'd left or why, but I could tell that it affected my mom in a painful way even though she tried to act like it didn't. She kept her composure as we scrolled through the photos, but I didn't. I'd completely fucking lost it, breaking down into tears before once again getting angry.

"No," I said, hating how disappointed she looked whenever I gave her that answer.

The problem was that I couldn't explain to anyone just how lost I truly felt and how the pictures didn't help. It was either remembering people that were no longer relevant or having no recollection of them at all. Everything proved as a reminder that I no longer knew who I was, who I had been, or what my life had been like.

The doorbell rang, and it caused me to jump.

"Don't worry. I'll get it," my mom offered, knowing full well that I had zero intention of answering it.

Whoever it was could stand out there forever for all I cared.

A chorus of voices reached me, and I stood up from the couch to see the people who were apparently my closest friends walking through the door. All five of them, looking like a walking billboard ad.

"Ryson, your friends are here," my mom announced, as if she couldn't see me standing there, eyeballing everyone.

"Hey," I said with a smile because it was really hard not to smile around this group of people.

My eyes scanned them all, stopping on Quinn for only a heartbeat longer than the rest but it was enough. I saw her expression shift, the hope that inflated inside her before I looked away. I hated giving her hope when I felt so hopeless.

"What are you guys doing here?" I asked as I moved back toward my spot on the couch and glanced at the TV.

"Wait. Are you watching baseball?" Quinn asked.

I instantly felt judged and out of place. *Was this some-thing I didn't usually do? Had Old Ryson not watched sports?*

"Yeah. I love it. I used to play, you know."

"When you were five!" my mom added from the kitchen

where she had started to fill up glasses.

"Still counts," I said, not wanting to argue, but Quinn's face held a curious expression. "What? Did I not watch baseball when we were together or something?"

"You thought it was boring. Didn't understand how anyone could sit through nine whole innings of it," she said with a shrug like she'd expected that whatever the old me had hated, the new me would too. But it clearly didn't work that way.

"Well, I like it now."

"You did throw out the first pitch once," Quinn said with a smile.

It jogged nothing in my brain. "I did? For what team?"

"The Dodgers."

I wished I could remember that. "How'd I do?" I asked, wondering if I'd embarrassed myself or not.

"You threw a strike." She laughed. "You're annoyingly good at everything you do, Ryson."

I shrugged it off but silently wondered if I still would be today. *Could I go outside and throw the ball like I used to?* I literally had no idea.

"I want to throw out the first pitch," one of the guys said as he plopped down next to me. "Tatum."

He extended his hand, and I shook it.

"I remember," I said before clarifying, "from the hospital, I mean. You're the one with the accent."

He laughed. "So y'all keep telling me," he countered, proving my point.

No one said much of anything after that. There was a lot

of staring at me while I stared at the TV before they all decided to sit down, Quinn noticeably keeping her distance. I glanced over at her to see if I could jog any particles of lost thoughts loose, but they all stayed firmly locked away. She caught me looking, and a soft smile appeared. I didn't return it. My mom brought out a tray of drinks, which interrupted the awkwardness, as she forced everyone to take one.

"Anyway, we all came here to see how you were and to talk to you about steps for moving forward," Madison, my agent, said.

I gave her an uninterested look. "Moving forward how?" I asked, taking a sip of the drink.

"It's already been a week since you left the hospital," she started, as if I didn't know that.

Did she think that I hadn't been keeping a running tally of the days? Because I had.

"And we've avoided the press, but they're starting to say some really unflattering things."

I knew instinctively that I should care more about what she was saying, but I was so disconnected to the life she was talking about that it was hard to have real feelings toward it.

"I saw some of the things," I admitted, blowing it off.

"You did?" Quinn asked, sounding shocked and hurt. "Which ones?"

"I don't know. Rumors about us breaking up. That sort of thing. I turned it off."

Quinn started blinking rapidly, clearly fighting back tears. Everything I did and said hurt this girl. I was constantly letting her down, and it didn't make me feel good.

"Do you have any interest in doing a joint interview?" Madison moved the conversation back on point.

"With who? Me and Quinn? The me I don't remember with the girl I don't either? That sounds like a great fucking idea."

"Hey, man, we know you're pissed, but—" the other guy in the group jumped in.

I knew he was only defending his girlfriend because I'd snapped at her, but I didn't care.

"You don't know anything. You have no idea how it feels to be me right now. No idea what it feels like to not remember a damn thing. I know I should look at you all and know who you are, but I don't. And you have memories of me that I don't have, and it makes me feel stupid, embarrassed, and lost. I hate it." I hadn't meant to snap at everyone, but it had been seven fucking days of the same shit. Seven disappointing mornings where I'd opened my eyes, hopeful, only to be let down again.

Madison placed a hand on her boyfriend's shoulder, instantly calming him down. "You're right. We don't know what it's like to be you. We only know what it's like to be us. And we all feel like we've lost you too." *This chick was good.* "So does the public. They need something."

"I don't want to do any interviews. I especially don't want to be on camera," I said, focusing my attention on Quinn. I hoped that she would understand or at least have my back even though I hadn't given her any reason to.

"That's fine," Madison said. "You don't have to. But that just means that Quinn's going to have to do it. And she's going to have to speak on your behalf. Are you okay with that?"

I continued looking at Quinn, wondering if I could trust her. *Had I trusted her when we were together? And if so, how much? With my life?* I wished I knew.

Quinn pushed off the couch and stood tall, her blonde hair spilling down her shoulders. "Can I talk to you?" She held out her hand toward me. "In private."

Ignoring her hand, I stood up and walked with her toward my back bedroom. Of course, she knew where it was. She had obviously been here before. I watched her move toward the bed and sit down.

"I can tell you have questions. Figured maybe you didn't want an audience."

I wondered for a moment how she knew before I remembered that we had been the *it* couple, as my Mom had called us. "Do you think this interview stuff is a good idea?"

She nodded. "Yeah, I do. I know you don't get it, but you and I are very well known. We have been in the public eye for years. Since we were kids. People are very invested in our personal lives. But since we've stayed quiet, the press has gotten antsy. They're printing things that I can't stay silent about anymore."

"About us?"

"About you," she said.

I could tell there was still so much about myself that I didn't know. But she obviously did. I wasn't in a state of mind to ask her about it either, not wanting to deal with the conversation that would ensue or to hear more things about me that I might not like.

"So, the old me would be okay with letting you speak for him? On his behalf, I mean."

A quick laugh escaped her lips. "In a heartbeat. Yes, he very much would have. And vice versa."

"So, we trusted each other?"

"Ryson," she breathed out, running her hands across her face. "We were a team."

"A good one?" I asked, still knowing nothing and piecing together information.

"The best. And I'm not just saying that." Her eyes scanned my room, and I saw the moment she noticed my cell phone, face down on my dresser. "Have you gone through your phone at all?"

"No," I lied, not wanting to tell her the truth.

"Are you planning to?"

"I'm not sure."

There had been moments when I was curious, but that curiosity had stopped the second I looked at a picture and felt no attachment to it but knew that I should have. I'd even read some text messages, but it was like reading a book written in an unfamiliar language. Nothing made sense. Nothing resonated.

"Don't you want to?" she asked, as her emotions started shifting. "Don't you want to see what your life used to look like?"

"Let me guess. It's full of pictures of us," I said, sounding like a dick because I had seen the gallery folders with Quinn's name on them. There was more than one.

"That wasn't what I meant, but I'm sure it is. I mean, we've been together for years. We've been in movies together. We live together. We're a fucking hashtag."

I looked at her, wondering what she was referring to. "I don't even know what that means … a hashtag?"

"Gah! You're so frustrating," she groaned as she threw her hands in the air and stood up, pacing back and forth.

"I don't know what you want me to say. You tell me you're my girlfriend, but I see a stranger when I look at you. What do you want from me? You want me to hug you and kiss you and tell you how much I've missed you? I can't do that."

She arched back like I'd slapped her, her eyes glossy. "I want you to give a shit that you don't remember. I want you to care that you feel nothing when you look at me. And I want you to *want* to remember," she said so honestly that her delivery almost felt like a blow to the head.

"Well, what I want"—I chose my words carefully and with intent—"is to not feel guilty that I don't."

Quinn stayed quiet for once. Maybe my words had struck a chord or finally made some kind of sense to her. Maybe she was finally understanding that the last thing I needed to add to this shitshow called my life was guilt.

The fact that she was waiting around for me to get better when I had no idea if I ever would or not made me feel like shit. I refused to let Quinn put her life on hold, to wait for my return to normalcy, when that very thing wasn't a guarantee. I couldn't be responsible for her happiness when I barely had any of my own.

Couldn't she see that I wanted to do what was best for her? Maybe she didn't see it that way at all.

"I'm just trying to do what's right here."

"And what do you think that is?"

"Letting you go. Setting you free. Not making you wait around for me," I said, feeling reasonable and logical in my argument.

She inhaled, the breath sharp and audible. "I don't want to be let go. I don't want to be set free. I want to be with you. The new you. The old you. I don't care. Don't you want to try to get to know each other again?"

It was a valid question. One I hadn't anticipated and wasn't sure how to answer.

"Maybe this version of you could love me too."

"I don't know if that's possible."

I figured she'd have something else to say. Quinn rarely seemed to run out of words or fight, but I was wrong.

With a nod that looked like resignation, she walked out of my room, and I heard her announce, "Let's go," before a bunch of movement followed her demand.

My mom slipped into my room after the front door slammed shut. "Old Ryson would have killed you for the way you just talked to her."

I guessed we hadn't had any privacy after all.

"Old Ryson isn't here anymore, Mom. And New Ryson—*me*—doesn't want to give her false hope, okay?"

"You do know that your memory could still return, right? It could come back tomorrow or the next day. No one knows," she said.

I felt like a broken record, repeating the same sentiment over and over again. "Exactly, Mom. No one knows. It could come back, but it might not. They already thought it would. What if it never does? I don't want Quinn waiting and hoping for the old me to magically reappear one day. It's not realistic. And it's not fair. To either one of us." Just thinking about the pressure made me feel like I'd never be able to escape it.

"But what about her suggestion? Getting to know each other again doesn't sound like such a bad idea." She sat on my bed the way Quinn had just moments before, her hands folded in her lap.

My stomach twisted. "I don't think it's a good idea."

"Why not?"

"Because I have no interest in acting or being in the spot-light. I can't fathom being a part of that world, and if I dated Quinn again, I'd have to be." My mind reeled, spitting out more and more thoughts. "Everyone would know who I was, but I wouldn't know them. There would be no escape. I wouldn't be able to start over and be someone new if I stayed in the same place with the same people. How could I ever not be Ryson the actor if I still dated Quinn the actress?"

My mom stared at me for only a moment before nodding. "Well, hell, that makes a lot of sense."

"Does it?" I breathed out in relief, finally feeling less crazed and a little more understood.

My mother was a psychiatrist after all. *Shouldn't she have seen all these things coming before I had?*

"Of course it does. And as much as I hate it, I'm afraid

you might be right."

I'd had no idea how much I needed to hear that acceptance until it was said. My mom might not like the choices I was making, but she supported my decisions, and it made me feel a less alone. None of us knew what the future held, but if my proverbial ship was sinking, I wasn't going to take anyone under with me.

ULTIMATE BACKFIRE
Quinn

W E RODE IN silence back to Malibu. No one dared to say a thing after we left Ryson's house. I licked my emotional wounds as I tried to process everything that had just happened. My reason for seeing him—hoping to ignite some spark of recognition or to see some flicker of emotion on his face—had totally backfired. I'd been so sure that I could convince him to get to know me again or at least agree to wanting to, but he wasn't having any of it. And everyone had heard him say as much.

After reading numerous articles online about wives who had made their husbands fall back in love with them after similar situations—*who knew this was such a common thing?*—I'd figured I could do the same or at least try. But Ryson wasn't my husband, and he wasn't obligated to me in the same way that married couples were. Even though we'd always been a team, he didn't feel that sense of responsibility toward me anymore. I'd lost my other half, but Ryson had lost the whole of who he was.

Any hope I'd secretly held had been snuffed out the

second he started making decisions for me—telling me what would be best and how to live my life going forward without him. New Ryson made a lot of assumptions, and there would be no talking him out of it. He might not remember who he was, but his stubbornness was still intact.

I sat in the car, wishing he would come back to me the same way he had when we were younger. When I thought back on that day, it felt surreal, like something ripped from the pages of a fantasy novel, not something that had actually happened before. The images flooded my mind, the story playing out in my head as emotions poured through me. I realized that Ryson couldn't do this, couldn't flip through the sheets of our shared history and pull out reminders of our love. He couldn't access our story and see all the things we'd been through and just how hard we'd fought to be together. His mind couldn't prove to him how deeply he had loved me.

Twelve weeks went by in silence. Eighty-four days without a peep from Ryson. His absence from the tabloids was noticeable, palpable even, but as I walked toward my trailer after finishing a scene, the shadowed figure waiting for me outside my door was unmistakable.

"Ryson!" I sprinted toward his now-open arms as a giant grin spread across his handsome face.

He looked so good. Throwing myself into his arms, I held him like he might disappear altogether if I let go.

"You're going to squeeze me to death, woman," he choked out with a laugh.

"What are you doing here?" I asked with a lilt in my

voice that I knew matched the smile on my face. "When did you get out?"

He pointed toward my trailer door. "Can we talk?"

Nerves coursed through me. His tone worried me. Had he come to tell me we could only be friends? Had everything changed for him since being in rehab? *I had no idea, but I found my mind racing through worst-case scenarios as I moved toward the door of my trailer and pulled it open.* Had Ryson come to shatter my heart in person? *I really wished he had done it by text message or something far less personal. I really didn't want to have to stare into those dark brown eyes while he broke me apart.*

We stepped inside, and I asked, "You want something to drink? Water or soda?" *I was nervous, and I knew he could tell.*

"No, I'm okay. Sit, Quinn," *he directed and moved toward my small kitchenette table.*

I paused for only a moment before I followed his lead, taking the seat across from him, the wood table separating us like it once had all those months before.

We stared at each other for a handful of heartbeats, neither one of us speaking. I felt those beats everywhere—in my chest, in my throat, pounding in my ears. Waiting for him to say something was almost unbearable. I tried to read his thoughts, the expression on his face, but I came up empty.

When I thought I couldn't take a single second more of the silence, he spoke, "I came straight here." *His eyes dipped toward the table before rising to meet mine and holding steady.*

"*From rehab?*" *I asked stupidly.* Where else would he have come from?

"*I just got released this afternoon,*" *he added, and my heart bounced back to life.*

My entire face softened as I stared into his eyes, which still hadn't left mine. Ryson staring was a little unnerving; he was always so intense.

"*What's the matter, Quinn?*"

"*I thought you might have changed your mind,*" *I admitted.* "*About us. Or mostly, about me,*" *I said solemnly.* "*It says that you shouldn't be with anyone for at least a year.*" *I pushed the stack of printed papers toward him. I had copies everywhere—a set in my car, here in the trailer, and in my bedroom at home.* "*I thought that maybe after you were sober, your feelings might change. Or maybe they hadn't even been real in the first place.*"

That was my most debilitating fear once Ryson had left— the notion that maybe what he'd felt for me wasn't real in the first place. That maybe everything he'd thought was real was simply a side effect of the drugs. It was the last thing I wanted, but once the idea had crossed my mind, it'd buried itself there and left me questioning everything.

Admitting my fear out loud to him had almost taken the breath out of me.

His face twisted with something I couldn't recognize. He grabbed the sheets of paper I'd printed out and tossed them to the ground. I watched them scatter, landing in various parts of my trailer.

"*I know what the papers say. I know what they all say,*

Quinn. And I don't care. I could never change my feelings when it comes to you. It was real then. It's real now. You and I will always be real."

His hand reached across the table for mine, and I moved it toward him.

He intertwined our fingers together and squeezed. "You were all I saw when I was in there. My end goal was always you. I know I wasn't supposed to think like that in order to get better, but how could anyone blame me? You think I could ever get over a girl like you, Quinn Johnson? It's never going to happen."

I couldn't stop myself from smiling if I tried. No one had ever said anything so romantic to me before, not even in the scripts I'd read. This was better than any movie, better than any fiction novel. This was real, and it was mine.

"So, you're done with the drugs? Just like that?" I snapped my fingers, not meaning to come off unsupportive, but I was concerned for our potential future.

How bad had Ryson's drug habit really been? Would it continue to be an issue forever or something he had to fight against doing for the rest of his life?

"It was a brief moment for me, Quinn. A mistake," he said before moving from his side of the table and scooting next to me, our thighs pressing together as I tried to focus on his words instead of the fact that our bodies were touching. "A mistake I won't make again; I can promise you that."

Ryson's face was mere inches from my own, and my heart sputtered inside my chest with his penetrating gaze.

"You're done with them forever then?"

He knew I didn't want drugs in my life, and I couldn't imagine a time when my feelings would change.

A small smile played across his face as he wrapped an arm around my shoulders. "Yes, I'm done with them forever."

"You won't want to use again? How can you be sure? What if things get hard or go bad?"

His head shook vehemently. "I never did them before. I was stupid. And angry. So angry with my dad. I had no idea what I was getting into, and I trusted people I shouldn't have. I'll never let myself get out of control like that again."

God, I believed him. I really believed him and not just because I wanted to.

"I'll never do anything to risk losing you," he added, catching me off guard before his lips crushed against mine without warning.

My shock was quickly replaced with desire as need raced inside me. Our tongues touched before he nipped at my bottom lip with his teeth, and I let out a moan. Kissing Ryson without cameras rolling was what life had been made for. Our mouths opened and closed, our tongues pressing and pushing against the other.

I couldn't touch him enough. My hands dug into his back, and I pulled at him, wanting every inch of him as close to me as possible. His hands fisted my hair, tugging as I moaned, and I arched my neck in response. It was as if our mouths being fused together wasn't close enough for him. He wanted more, and I gave it. We breathed each other in, neither one willing to pull away as we moved in unison—tongues *dancing, spines tingling, the need for each other growing.*

I hadn't realized just how badly I wanted this with Ryson until it was happening. He'd made me a promise, and I'd silently been counting on him to deliver. I'd tried to convince myself for weeks that I'd survive if he never showed up, but I had known even then that it was a lie.

He gently pulled away from me, and I breathed out, "I can't believe you really came for me."

"I told you I would."

"I know, but—" I started to say before he cut me off.

"No buts, Quinn. I meant what I said to you, and I always will. Always. It's you and me now. Say it," he demanded, and even though I was only sixteen, I knew that this was one of those life-defining moments I'd never forget. "Say it, Quinn."

I didn't even have to think twice. I wanted to be with him. "It's you and me, Ryson."

"Forever," he added with a cocky grin.

"How do you know?" I asked.

His grin quickly fell. "How do I know what?"

"That it's forever?"

"Because this"—he placed his hand on his chest right over his heart before doing the same to mine—"isn't something you just find every day. The way I feel about you"—he moved his hand back over his heart—"it's not puppy love. It's not fleeting. I know people would probably say we're too young to know whether or not it's forever, Quinn, but I know. I want you today. I'll want you tomorrow. I'll want you fifty years from now."

I found myself swallowing hard and fighting back tears as his hand cupped my cheek.

"Forever, Quinn."

"And then some," I added a line of my own, and his grin reappeared.

The car slammed on the brakes, and I jolted back to the present, my seat belt pressing against my shoulder.

"Fucking paparazzi. Move!" Walker shouted, and I knew we were back home.

I pulled out my phone and typed in a code, opening the gates as Walker waited before parking in the driveway.

"At least there aren't ten thousand of them here any-more." Paige rolled her eyes.

I looked out the window, realizing that she was right. The number of paparazzi had definitely reduced, and I briefly wondered why. *Had something bad happened to another celebrity? I hoped not.*

"Yeah, but if they aren't here, where are they?" Madison asked, echoing my silent sentiment.

We piled out of Walker's SUV and headed inside, ignoring the shouts and questions from outside the gates. The press outside my house might have dwindled in numbers since we first left, but the desire for answers hadn't. And even though Madison had her cell phone on silent, we all saw how often it rang.

I led us through the entryway and into the kitchen before taking a seat at the table. "Okay, so we need to figure out a plan," I said as everyone helped themselves to drinks from the fridge and sat around the table.

It was clear that something needed to be said, and Ryson obviously couldn't be the one to say it.

"Are we not going to talk about what just happened?" Tatum asked, his Southern twang in full effect.

He was worried about me. They all were.

Lifting my arms, I asked, "What do you want to talk about?"

"We heard what Ryson said," Tatum added, and they all stared at me with sad expressions and even sadder eyes.

"Which is why we need to figure out what we're doing since he has no interest in being involved."

"That's not what I meant," Tatum said.

I gave him a shrug. "I know."

"How are you feeling?" Paige asked. It was the million-dollar question at the moment.

How was I feeling?

"I don't know." It was an honest answer. My emotions seemed to flip around, switching from one extreme to the other with each breath I took. "I think I'm doing a lot of compartmentalizing right now. I want to deal with the press and how we're going to handle them first. Ryson and his stubborn ass second."

That garnered a few laughs.

Madison pulled out her phone, her fingers working wildly over the screen as her face pinched. "Okay, I've made a very small list of people I think will be best to have a sit-down interview with. It's going to be a prime-time slot. There's no way around that. They are going to want huge ratings and will most likely center million-dollar advertising campaigns around it. So, if you turn on the television, Quinn, you're going to see the interview advertised nonstop until it airs. Understood?"

"Yeah, I get it. I know how this works."

"I know you do, but you've never been in a situation quite like this before."

"I understand," I said, knowing that Madison would never put me in something she thought I couldn't handle.

"I was also thinking that we should do a group exclusive with a trusted magazine and maybe a couple of online blogs. We would make sure we had editorial approval before they printed anything, online or otherwise."

"Will they agree to that?" Tatum asked.

"They will if they want the interview," Madison remarked, and Tatum complimented her badassery.

I raised my hand like we were in class and waited for Madison to call on me. "Do you think we should be giving online blogs and bloggers exclusive content? Maybe it'd be a better idea if we handled anything online ourselves and posted the information directly on our websites. That way, the bloggers wouldn't be making any more money off of us. They wouldn't have anything on their sites that the everyday person couldn't find by going to our individual websites. Does that make sense?"

"That's actually a great idea," Madison said with a smile. "I wasn't thinking about it like that, but that's good."

"Old Ryson would have loved that idea," Walker said before smacking his mouth closed like he'd said something wrong.

"It's okay. He would have. He would have been laughing his ass off right now at us pulling one over on them," I said with a smile.

"He would totally have approved of this," Madison agreed. "But I still think we should do a group interview with a print magazine. They could use portions of that interview on their online site, of course, but that would be it."

"I think that's good. I also really like the idea of the magazine being all five of us together."

"To clarify, the on camera should just be you," Madison added, her tone sincere.

"I know," I agreed, and that was how we got the ball rolling.

The group of us tackled each one of Madison's interview options before deciding on a woman who was known for being fair and honest. She had actually cried during more than one of her interviews, but that was part of what made her so captivating and charming to watch. Carolina French came across the television screen like a real person, as opposed to some hardened, robotic, unemotional journalist.

"I'll make sure I get a list of potential questions from her before we film. We'll go through them together and get rid of anything you aren't comfortable answering. I can also give her parameters to start with, so she doesn't stray off topic. It's the best we can hope for during a live interview.

Madison was back in full-on work mode, and I loved her for it. It kept my mind distracted. Even though the main topic was still my and Ryson's relationship, it felt more like work instead of my broken heart.

I shook my head. "I'd actually like to hear what questions she has before we give her lines not to cross. It will be interesting to hear what people want to know. It might help us decide what we put online."

"Again"—Madison held out her hand toward me— "Quinn for the win."

"Please don't start that hashtag," I groaned, hating the whole rhyming thing that people did.

Madison pushed back from the table. "I'll work on getting this scheduled. And I'll set up an interview for all of us with the magazine. And, yeah"—she shrugged—"that's all for now."

"Sounds good," everyone agreed, and I realized that they were all going to leave.

I was apparently good at compartmentalizing when I was with a group, but once I was alone, I knew I'd lose myself in the past memories and my present heartache. Ryson didn't want to be with me anymore. It was a fact that could no longer be denied or avoided.

And soon, the entire world would know it too.

FINDING A NEW NORMAL
Ryson

AFTER QUINN AND the group had left the other day, I
hadn't felt relieved like I'd figured I would. I'd honestly
thought that admitting the truth to Quinn instead of avoiding
it and her would make me feel better. But ever since that day,
I'd been feeling uneasy and on edge, and I had no idea why.

No matter what I'd said to Quinn or admitted out loud to
my mom, there was a part of me that very much still hoped
I'd get my memories back. No one in their right mind would
willingly choose this hell.

The doctors had told me over the phone yesterday that
this wasn't entirely normal but to not give up hope. The tone
of their voices told me what they didn't—that I should have
already gotten my memories back by now and they were
concerned. Have you ever noticed that doctors are pretty
shitty liars?

I really wanted to remember my life, but so far, that
hadn't happened. Every morning when my eyes opened and
my brain snapped into place, it was the same thing—blank
spaces and holes where the people and places I had known

were supposed to be instead. I started believing that the old me might never come back.

"Hey, honey," my mom said as she walked through the front door, a bag of groceries in her arms. I stood up to help her, but she waved me back. "It's only one bag. I've got it."

She had recently started leaving me alone during the day for a few hours at a time, so she could see her patients. I'd had to practically force her out the door that first day, asking her what she thought I was going to do or where she thought I'd go in her absence. She'd finally admitted that she didn't want me to be alone. She was scared that I might be depressed.

Guessed I wasn't so great of an actor after all. Of course I was depressed, but I hadn't wanted her to notice.

"How was work?"

"Good. Tiring." She shot me a quick look, and I knew better than to ask her detailed questions about her clients. Patient-doctor confidentiality and all that. "I thought I'd make Grandma's famous fish and chips for dinner."

I offered a noncommittal shrug. "Sounds good. I liked it before?"

"It was one of your favorites," she said before stopping short, her hand on her hip. "But maybe you might not like it anymore?"

"I guess we'll find out," I said with a laugh.

She nodded as she finished unloading the food, pulling out various mixing bowls and ingredients. "I guess we will. What'd you do while I was gone?" She puttered around in the kitchen, trying to appear nonchalant when I knew that she was digging for insight.

My mom didn't want me to feel like she was pushing too hard or treating me like one of her clients, so she tried to pretend like her questions were no big deal when I knew she was mentally filing them into some category that only made sense to her.

"I was making a list of questions," I said, catching her off guard as I held up a pad of paper in the air.

"Really? What kind of questions?"

Glancing at the list, I started reading them all off, "I wanted to know what used to interest me. And not acting, I mean. What was I like as a kid? What did I do? Did I like pets? Did I like sports? What did you think I was going to be before I became an actor?"

"That's a good question." She looked almost perplexed as she coated the fish with some sort of breading mixture. "You've been acting for so long; I'm not sure I ever imagined you doing anything else. And when you were little, it was the typical thing that most boys said they wanted to be."

She paused, and I waited for her to continue.

When she didn't fill in the blanks, I asked, "Which was what?"

"Sorry. Um, you know, fireman, police officer, professional baseball player. That kind of thing."

All things that didn't pique my interest as she rattled them off.

"What else did I used to do?"

She stopped messing with the fish and wiped her hands

on a dish towel, facing me. "Ryson, honey, you've been acting since you were a kid. You've been famous almost your whole life. Your dreams and aspirations have changed as you've gotten older, but they were still all entertainment industry–based. I know what you hoped to do outside of acting, but it still wasn't a normal, everyday occupation like you're looking for right now."

"I wanted to stop acting?" I asked through my surprise.

"Well, yeah," she offered like I should have known that already. "You wanted to start directing. Quinn mentioned something about writing too, but you'd never said anything to me." She sounded almost wistful.

I found myself nodding because … writing. It struck a chord.

"That reality show I told you about in the hospital. Do you remember?"

I nodded.

"You were so excited and proud because you'd fought really hard to be able to tell your story in an honest way. It was going to be your directorial debut. And you were going to have editorial control over it as well. It was a pretty big deal."

"And now, it's not happening?"

"You know, I don't really know," she said as she started peeling potatoes. "But I can't imagine that they'd want to do it without you."

"So, I haven't just ruined my own life, but everyone else's too," I mumbled under my breath.

"You haven't ruined anyone's life, Ryson. Changed

things, sure. But ruined, no."

"But you just said this thing we were working for isn't going to happen now."

"None of your friends need that show. They agreed to do it because you'd asked. It was your idea. This doesn't change their lives at all."

I actually believed her. "Okay. Thanks, Mom. I still wish I knew what else I'd wanted to do with my life."

"Well, lucky for you, you don't have to decide right this second."

She was right. I didn't have to figure out what I wanted to be today or even tomorrow.

We had gone through my finances the other morning, and my eyes had almost shot out of my head when I saw the amount of money I had to my name. It was fucking crazy. If I wanted to, I could live off of that money for the rest of my life and never lift a finger again. But I didn't want to.

"You want to know what I'd suggest to you if you were one of my patients?"

"What?"

"I'd tell you to start keeping a journal. To write it all down—your feelings, your emotions, everything."

"That's a good idea," I said, not wanting to tell her that I'd already started doing that.

"I have a bunch of blank journals in the top drawer of my desk," she said with a smile.

I walked away to go grab one even though I'd already taken three.

I'd started writing the first night we came back with no

plan or motive in mind; I just knew that I needed to get the thoughts out of my head, and writing seemed the best way to do that. It was the only thing that made me feel even remotely better. The journals didn't judge me or get their feelings hurt. I could be as cruel as I wanted with my pen, and no one would be the wiser because I never planned on sharing them with anyone.

When I walked back into the living room, the air smelled delicious.

"Holy shit, that smells good."

"Fried fish."

AFTER EATING GRANDMA'S famous fish and chips—which were French fries and not potato chips like I had wrongfully assumed—I dubbed the meal still one of my favorites. My mom grinned from ear to ear as she shoved me out of the kitchen. I tried to help clean, but she wasn't having any of it.

I sat down on the couch, one of my journals in hand. I opened it to the next blank page and wrote the date and time at the top. It had become a habit of mine, to include the time of my entries, just in case I saw a pattern emerge. For example, did I tend to be angrier and more bitter at night, or was it first thing in the morning? So far, my emotions had been all over the place, and the time of day had nothing to do with it.

My mom stepped into the living room and turned on the television, talking into the remote. It listened and went to the channel she'd asked for. Quinn's face appeared, and my entire body tensed.

"What is this?" I asked my mom as she took a seat next to me, the remote gripped in her hand.

She turned the volume up. "Quinn's live interview. I want to watch it."

Well, I didn't. I didn't want to fucking watch it at all, but I found myself unable to move, my eyes and ears glued to the screen as Quinn stared back, her face looking pained, even through all the makeup.

INTERVIEWER: I THINK THE BIG QUESTION WE ALL WANT TO KNOW IS, WHERE EXACTLY IS RYSON?

QUINN: HE'S RECOVERING AT HOME WITH HIS MOM.

INTERVIEWER: SO, HE'S NOT IN REHAB THEN?

"Why the hell would I be in rehab?" I asked, shooting my mom a glare, but she was too focused on Quinn to notice.

QUINN: NO. HE'S NOT IN REHAB. I WANT TO MAKE IT VERY CLEAR THAT RYSON DOES NOT HAVE A DRUG PROBLEM.

INTERVIEWER: I UNDERSTAND THAT YOU'RE UPSET, BUT YOU CAN'T BLAME PEOPLE FOR WONDERING. I MEAN, WITH HIS PAST DRUG USE AND EVERYTHING.

QUINN: I CAN THOUGH. I CAN BLAME PEOPLE FOR WONDERING. RYSON HASN'T TOUCHED DRUGS IN YEARS, AND THERE'S NO REA-SON FOR ANYONE TO THINK OTHERWISE. IT WAS AN EASY HEADLINE TO CREATE. A CHEAP SHOT TO TAKE TO MAKE MONEY.

INTERVIEWER: OKAY. SO THEN, IF HE'S NOT IN REHAB, WHY DIDN'T

HE GO HOME WITH YOU?

This question clearly struck even more of a nerve. Quinn looked more uncomfortable than I'd ever seen her. She swallowed hard, her eyes starting to well with tears.

QUINN: BECAUSE HE DOESN'T REMEMBER ME.

INTERVIEWER: THE RUMORS OF HIS AMNESIA ARE TRUE?

QUINN: THEY ARE.

INTERVIEWER: DOES HE REMEMBER ANYTHING?

QUINN: NO.

The interviewer let out a small gasp, as though she was surprised by this news. For all I knew, maybe she was. I wanted to get up and walk out of the room, but I couldn't. It was a surreal thing to realize that these people were talking about me.

INTERVIEWER: I WANT TO ASK YOU SOMETHING ELSE, QUINN. IT'S A LITTLE UNCOMFORTABLE, BUT I HEARD YOU TWO WERE FIGHTING THE DAY OF HIS SURFING ACCIDENT.

My ears perked up at this little tidbit of information. *We had been fighting? How come no one had said anything? I'd thought we were some perfect couple who never had any issues.*

QUINN: I HAVE NO IDEA HOW YOU HEARD THAT, BUT, YES, IT'S TRUE.

INTERVIEWER: WHAT WAS IT ABOUT, IF YOU DON'T MIND ME ASK-ING?

Quinn let out a laugh that made me shift in my seat as I waited for her response.

QUINN: GETTING MARRIED.

INTERVIEWER: GETTING MARRIED?

QUINN: I WANTED TO GET ENGAGED AND MARRIED AT SOME POINT, BUT RYSON DIDN'T.

Say what? I hadn't wanted to get married? Since when?

I looked at my mom, but her expression told me that she had known all of this already.

"I forgot to tell you about the fight. I'm sorry," she said. "It slipped my mind."

"Is it true?"

"I guess. Quinn said that you didn't believe in it."

That shocked me even more. "What? I didn't believe in marriage?" I felt like I believed in marriage now. *Why wouldn't I have believed in it then?*

"That's what she said you told her. I was just as shocked as you are."

"Do we know why? I feel like that's wrong," I said, shaking my head.

"I can only assume it has to do with me and your father, but you never talked to me about it."

We kept discussing the topic a little while longer, both of us tuning out the interview until a question dragged us back at the same time.

INTERVIEWER: WHAT WILL YOU DO? HOW WILL YOU MOVE ON?

QUINN: I DON'T KNOW. HOW DO YOU MOVE ON FROM SOMETHING
LIKE THIS?

INTERVIEWER: IT'S ALMOST LIKE HE DIED IN A WAY.

QUINN: YOU'RE NOT WRONG.

INTERVIEWER: WE'LL NEVER SEE HIM ACT AGAIN?

QUINN: I DON'T THINK SO.

I clearly had not grasped the scope of what Quinn and I had been, not only to each other, but to the public as well. It all seemed so weird to me—this level of involvement in our personal lives, the way the interviewer looked genuinely disappointed with Quinn's answers. I swore, I had even seen her tear up a time or two.

INTERVIEWER: ARE YOU SAYING THAT RYSON DOESN'T WANT TO BE
WITH YOU?

QUINN: NOT ANYMORE.

INTERVIEWER: DID HE SAY THAT?

QUINN: HE DOESN'T REMEMBER WHO HE IS OR WHO I AM. HE
DOESN'T WANT ANYTHING TO DO WITH THIS LIFE.

INTERVIEWER: OR YOU.

QUINN: OR ME.

INTERVIEWER: QUINN, YOU'RE BREAKING MY HEART HERE.

QUINN: TELL ME ABOUT IT.

INTERVIEWER: I THINK I SPEAK FOR THE WHOLE COUNTRY WHEN I
SAY THAT THIS IS SOMETHING WE NEVER SAW COMING.

QUINN: BECAUSE IT WASN'T COMING. IT WASN'T SUPPOSED TO END LIKE THIS FOR US.

INTERVIEWER: HOW IS THIS EVEN POSSIBLE?

QUINN: I ASK MYSELF THAT EVERY DAY.

"Turn it off," I said to my mom, who still held the remote in her hand. "I don't want to see this anymore. Mom, turn it off."

She did as I'd asked, her face solemn. "What's wrong?"

"Nothing," I yelled before stalking off into my bedroom and slamming the door closed.

I hated having so many emotions running through me at once.

I reached for my phone and fired off a text to Quinn before thinking better of it. It was the first time I had used my phone to send anyone a text since the accident.

SAW YOUR INTERVIEW. WISH YOU HADN'T SAID ALL THAT. I THOUGHT YOU SAID I COULD TRUST YOU.

She apparently didn't like that, since her response read;

FUCK OFF, RYSON.

I guessed she had a lot of emotions running through her too.

But I wondered, *Is that the way we talk to each other? Am I supposed to be offended or find it funny, or is she really pissed off at me?*

Unsure of it all, I typed out a response.

YOU MADE ME SOUND LIKE A HEARTLESS VILLAIN! MAYBE THAT WAS YOUR PLAN ALL ALONG? TO GET EVERYONE ON THE QUINN VICTIM TRAIN? WHAT DO THEY SAY? ANY PUBLICITY IS GOOD PUBLICITY? HAVE A NICE LIFE.

ARE YOU KIDDING ME RIGHT NOW? JESUS, RYSON, ALL I DID WAS TELL THE TRUTH! SORRY IF YOU DON'T LIKE HEARING IT. NO ONE FORCED YOU TO WATCH.

I threw my phone across the room. I had known texting her was a mistake. I wouldn't be making it again.

THE FALLOUT
Quinn

HEARTLESS VILLAIN? A villain?

New Ryson was a total jackass. But I still loved him. And I hated myself for it. Okay, I didn't really hate myself for loving him, but why couldn't my heart get the memo that even though he still looked like the Old Ryson we had known and loved, he was no longer that man?

"You did great, Quinn. Really great," Madison said as she ushered me from the studio and into the back of our waiting car. The interview had ended twenty minutes earlier, but I spent time thanking Carolina and signing a few items for an upcoming charity auction she was hosting.

"Ryson didn't think so." I handed her my phone, so she could read our text exchange.

"He just doesn't know how any of this works anymore. He's not the same person we used to know. I'll talk to him and calm him down." She sounded exasperated and tired.

"Please don't call him while I'm in the car," I said, practically begging. The last thing I needed to hear was her trying to make him feel better while I was currently spinning out in a plethora of unearthed feelings and emotions.

"I wouldn't." She placed a hand on my shoulder before quickly typing into her phone and smiling as the driver continued down the Pacific Coast Highway and toward my house. "You're trending on Twitter. Multiple hashtags for you and the interview. Front-page placement on Yahoo, Bing, and Microsoft News."

"Are they saying good or bad things?" I wondered.

Her face suddenly turned crimson. "Mostly good," she said.

I leaned toward her, trying to peek over her shoulder at her phone. She angled it away.

"There're a couple of things you don't need to see," she suggested rather forcefully, and all it did was pique my interest and make me want to know more.

"Like what? Are they calling me names? I'm going to see it all sooner or later."

"Don't say I didn't warn you," she said before turning her screen completely toward me, so I could read the newest, trending hashtags.

#TheThingsIdDoToRysonMiller
#RysonIsSingle
#BreaksupsAreGoodForBusiness
#MarryMeRyson

"Madison, tell me talking wasn't the wrong thing to do. Tell me I did the right thing." I looked at her through pleading eyes. *Had I just made the biggest mistake of my life by telling the world that he and I were over?*

I'd never imagined Ryson loving someone who wasn't me, but of course, he would. Time would pass, he would date someone new, and I'd have to hear all about it. The whole world would. No matter if Ryson didn't want to be in the spotlight anymore, he was never going to be able to avoid it. Cameras would follow him for the rest of his life, regardless of what that life held.

"The truth would have come out eventually. And who knows how they would have spun it? You did the right thing by talking."

The car pulled to a hard stop in front of my house, and I reached for my keys. "It doesn't feel like it right now. You don't need to come in. I'll just talk to you later," I said.

Madison looked shocked. She hadn't expected me to ditch her once we got home, but I was in no mood to discuss business anymore. I had to deal with the fallout of my heart and the fact that it had truly lost its home.

Ignoring the paparazzi outside, I walked slowly toward my front door. I wasn't sure what was expected of me at this point. *Was I just supposed to forget about Ryson altogether?* Just because he no longer remembered the life we'd once shared, I still did. It was like I'd told Carolina during our interview—this was a level of pain and rejection no one could imagine.

I felt like I was stuck in an old *Buffy the Vampire Slayer* episode. Or maybe it was the spin-off, *Angel*? Where one of them remembered the love they'd shared and the other one had had their memory wiped clean. That was my life now.

And it wasn't fair.

It was torture.

How had he and I made it through everything we did as kids, but we couldn't find a way to make it through this? What was the point of getting through all of that if we were only going to end up here, apart? Maybe we'd already used up our second chance. We had gotten it all those years ago, and it was possible that people didn't get to have another. Maybe second chances only happened once in a lifetime.

I'd gone on live television and bared my heart and soul to anyone watching. I'd thought I was doing the right thing by standing up for Ryson. I put a hard end to the rumors about his drug use, and I set the record straight, hoping it meant that they would all back off and give him space.

But all I'd really done was make it open season on Ryson. He was fair game now, and I was the one who had made sure they all knew it.

★ ★ ★

WEEKS HAD PASSED since *the interview that rocked the celebrity world.* That was what everyone referred to it as. I deemed it as the opening act to my own personal hell.

Some days were easier than others. Some were definitely worse. There was no telling what might trigger me. I would be perfectly fine, but then I'd walk into the corner store, see Ryson's favorite brand of chips, and break down crying in aisle five. There was no rhyme or reason for my behavior.

At times, I felt like a ticking bomb, set to explode without warning. No one knew when it would come, not even me.

But for the most part, I got better. It might not seem like it from an outsider's perspective, but internally, I knew the truth; I was making it through. The good days started to outnumber the bad. That was progress.

I tried to accept the fact that Ryson would never love me again. That our lives would go on and that they no longer included one another, but I hated every single second of it. It felt unnatural. It went against all my instincts.

I didn't know how to make my heart stop loving him or how to make my soul stop reaching out for his. My mind never stopped craving his intellect, my body constantly missing his touch. Even in dreams, I was trying to get to him, but he remained out of reach.

Paige tried to get me to start writing, but writing had always been more of Ryson's thing than mine. I placated her one afternoon after she showed up with a beautifully engraved notebook in hand. She said if I wrote out my thoughts, fears, and emotions while I was experiencing them, it would help me heal. I asked her if she had been talking to Ryson's mom because it sounded like something a psychiatrist would say, and she turned bright red. I couldn't even be mad at her for it. I knew she was only trying to help.

I learned quickly that I hated writing by hand, my fingers cramping and my thoughts coming in quicker than I could ever get them out with a pen. Instead, I found myself typing away night after night on my laptop, putting entries in a file folder I'd labeled Fantasy Football for no good reason whatsoever. It wasn't like I had anything to hide. Or anyone to hide it from.

"We could put all your journal entries into a book, you know," Paige announced seemingly out of nowhere from the lounge chair next to mine.

We sat outside and soaked up the sun. It felt like it was the first time that I was able to allow the sun to touch me without cursing her existence. If she was going to move on and continue doing her job, I needed to as well. Stupid sun.

"I'm not selling my most private thoughts," I bit back, feeling a little more life creeping in. I'd felt alone, in a dark cave of emotions, for so long that it was scary coming all the way back out. But I knew that I needed to. It was time.

"We could edit them first. If I wasn't your best friend, I'd buy that book. I'd want to know every single thing you thought."

"You wouldn't be the only one." I pretended to sound bored.

The press still wanted more. Even after the tell-all live interview and our group magazine one. It hadn't been enough. It would never be enough. If there was one more sentence that they could squeeze out of us in regard to Ryson and this situation, they wanted access to it.

"People are just curious. They want to know how you feel. They want to hear it. From you. I mean, you get that, right?"

"I do," I said because I did. I understood it. I always had. "But I don't want to give it to them. I've already given them enough."

That was part of the truth. The rest was that I knew it would be all for him. That if I ever did write a book and publish it, it would be for the sole purpose of having Ryson read it. But knowing New Ryson, he'd never even crack the spine.

"You have," Paige agreed. "Okay, this is going to be weird, but I have to tell you." She clasped her hands together.

"You're making me nervous."

"No, it's nothing like that." She tried to wave me off. "It's just that I ran into Liam yesterday."

"Liam Lanter?" I asked, knowing full well that it had to be him. We didn't know any other Liams who ran in our celebrity circle.

"Yeah."

"Okay? And?"

"He asked about you."

"So?" I all but blurted out. "I assume that everyone we've ever met in the history of our careers has asked about me lately."

"I mean that he asked, *asked* about you. Like, I think he's interested in you. In a *more than just a caring friend* kind of way, if you catch my drift," she kept talking.

I had caught her drift from the start, so I wished she'd stop.

"Interested in me?" The words came out sounding horrified.

It wasn't that Liam wasn't a hot commodity or a really good-looking guy with a stellar reputation in the business. It was that I had been so concerned over the idea of Ryson dating someone new that it never occurred to me that someone eventually might want to date me.

"Ryson isn't the only one who's single again, you know."

"Is it idiotic that I never even thought about that?" I might be ready to start putting my life back together, but I definitely wasn't ready to date, and I had no idea when I would be.

"No. But it's something to consider. Guys are going to want to date you, Quinn. You haven't been available for years. There's probably a line outside the gates right now."

"Speaking of," I said, referring to the gates outside the house, "there's something I have to tell you too." Through a long breath, I pulled myself up into a sitting position, my legs swinging over.

Paige mimicked my pose. "Sounds serious."

"It's about the house."

"This house?" she asked, her voice cracking.

"I called a realtor that Madison recommended yesterday. She's coming to look at it tomorrow."

"You're selling?" She actually looked crestfallen.

"I can't stay here, Paige. I don't know how to move forward if I keep living in the past."

"Are you sure, *sure*? It's only been a couple of months," she said.

It hurt to know that everyone could classify my time apart from Ryson so flippantly, as if it'd passed without pain.

"I know. But you say a *couple of months* like it's this quick blip of time," I said, snapping my fingers. "But for me, it's been sixty days of torture."

Living here without Ryson wasn't living at all. It was too hard—too many memories, too many ghosts lurking around every corner. Selling the house would be the first step in reclaiming my new life. I'd been living on pause in the months since Ryson's accident, and I couldn't live that way anymore. It was time that I acknowledged the truth—he wasn't coming back.

And it wasn't his fault. It wasn't anyone's fault. And I had to stop being so angry with him for it or feeling sad for all we'd lost. It was time to find who I was without him. It wouldn't be easy, but it needed to be done; otherwise, I'd waste the rest of my life away, and I deserved more than that. Old Ryson would have never wanted me to spend my life in misery, surrounded by what-ifs and if-onlys.

Paige wistfully looked around the yard. "I love this house."

"I do too."

"You're sure this is the right thing to do? You don't want to get something temporary and see how you feel in six months or a year?"

I knew that Paige believed that if more time passed, I'd eventually change my mind or accept the idea of living here alone. But the thing was, the more time that passed, the worse I felt, and the less that I could accept building a life in this home without him in it.

"I'm sure."

"Where will you go?"

"I don't know yet. Maybe inland? Bel Air? Toluca Lake? Somewhere closer to the studios, so I don't have to drive so damn far."

"It will be weird, not coming to Malibu to hang out."

"At least Walker and Madison still live here, so we don't have to quit it altogether."

"It's not the same though," she said.

I knew she was right. Whether it was because Paige had been there during the buying process or not, there was something special about this house.

"I know." I offered her a small smile.

She dropped her sunglasses over her eyes and lay back down on the lounger. "I wouldn't be able to stay here either if it were me and Tatum. Just in case you were wondering."

"I wasn't." I let out a laugh, and for the first time in what felt like forever, I *knew* ... that it was all going to be okay.

That, at some point, *I* was going to be okay.

FEELING SORRY FOR MYSELF
Ryson

I WAS IN a rut. The days and hours passed, and nothing changed. I hadn't left the house and still had no idea what I wanted to do with the rest of my life. I was no closer to any answers than I had been my first day here.

I'd cut myself off from everyone, except my mother, and that in itself was depressing. I needed to get back out there. To where exactly, I had no idea, but I needed to at least start figuring it out. My new life was waiting for me to begin living it, and instead, I'd been ignoring it, hoping it would miraculously create itself.

"I had a long talk with your doctors today," my mother announced.

I hadn't even heard her come in the house.

"Why?" I asked, annoyed that my mom was the one talking to them instead of them talking to me.

"Because I feel like you've given up." My mom rounded the corner, her voice stern and annoyed.

"Why are you so mad right now?"

"Because you're just accepting this and not even trying to

fix what you had. You're avoiding everyone you knew. You won't look at pictures. You won't even touch your phone. It's like you don't want to remember."

"If it was that easy, don't you think I would have done it by now?"

"I don't know. Maybe you like your new life of sitting on my couch and pouting like a damn five-year-old."

Well, that was brutal. "I'll get out of your hair then, Mom. I have more than enough money to get my own place."

I stood up and took two steps before she reached me and yanked on my arm.

"Sit down," she said, pointing back at the couch.

I did what she'd demanded because, to be honest, a pissed off Mom was scary as hell.

"You're going to sit here and watch this with me until it's done. Do you hear me?"

"Watch what?"

My mom pointed at the TV as it turned on, and a younger version of myself and Quinn appeared on the screen. I moved to stand up and storm out of the room the same way I had after Quinn's interview, but my Mom's voice stopped me cold.

"Sit your ass down and watch this, or I'll handcuff you to the chair."

I shot her a look, not liking being told what to do, but listening anyway. Like I'd said, scary. As. Hell. Chuffing out a breath, I sat begrudgingly and hoped to God this wouldn't hurt too much—either from the disappointment of not jogging my memory or seeing my unrecognizable face staring back at me.

I was going to stop the drugs. I needed something else to focus my attention on. It couldn't be Quinn—I knew that—but I also felt like something was going to have to take their place in order for me to get through this. I was starting to worry that maybe I had some sort of addictive personality disorder, always needing to chase a high to feel content. The worst part was that I hadn't been like this before I did drugs for the first time. There had never been this overwhelming void inside of me, just begging to be filled. I had been utterly normal. It was like the drugs had shaken up my insides and rearranged everything, throwing it all off-balance. I hated it.

Glancing around my trailer, my eyes landed on a banged-up surfboard propped up against the wall. It had been sitting there for so long that I stopped seeing it. I'd played a surfer in my last movie and fallen in love with the sport after I insisted on filming my own water scenes. Well, most of them anyway. There was no way in hell that I could ride the kinds of waves those guys cut through with ease. That took years of practice, and I'd been on a board for about two and a half months, tops.

I had taken lessons from the best pro surfers in the area. I studied the water, wave breaks, and reef placement. I practiced harder than anyone else because I wanted my work to look authentic. The only way I was giving the okay for a stunt double in any of the water scenes was if I couldn't make it look good myself. And, apparently, I had done all right because the majority of me actually surfing made the final *cuts instead of the cutting room floor.*

I remembered how proud I'd been of my hard work and how much I'd loved being in the water, searching for a wave to catch. It was calming, almost meditative, floating there, being at one with something so vast.

How could I have forgotten that?

Reaching for the blue-and-white board, I pulled it free from its clips and leaned it up against my table. After we wrapped for the night, I was going to strap this baby to my car and hit the water ASAP.

If the ocean didn't help kill me, maybe it could save me.

What the hell was that? A scene from this movie? A scene from my life?

"Mom, stop the movie. Stop the movie!" I shouted, my body trembling.

She pressed a button, and my face, as I held Quinn's in the palm of my hand while I looked at her like she'd hung the damn moon, was paused on the big screen.

"I think I remembered something."

IT'S TIME
Quinn

AFTER TALKING TO Paige the other day, I'd been feeling better about everything. About my decisions, my state of mind, and life in general. I really had accepted the fact that Ryson wasn't ever going to remember us, something I'd sworn I'd never be able to do for as long as I lived and breathed. After the interview, it'd all seemed easier somehow. It'd felt like as long as we had kept Ryson's memory loss a secret, we could pretend it wasn't really happening. Once the cat had gotten out of the bag, so to speak, true healing had begun.

I'd talked to Ryson's mom briefly about selling our house, and she agreed that it was probably the best decision for both of us. She mentioned a clean slate, starting fresh, and then she cried. I'd stayed strong while we were on the phone, but the second I'd ended the call, I'd lost it and grieved for the future mother-in-law I was never going to have. It was amazing how much one life could be wrapped up in another's. How intertwined all of our individual pieces could become.

My real estate agent, Jules, told me that the house would most likely sell within the first week, and my gut instincts told me that she was right and wasn't just BS'ing me. She seemed genuine and not arrogant like a lot of real estate agents in the area tended to be. Malibu was always a hot market, and since our house was celebrity-owned, it only added to the appeal. I knew the second I decided to list it, things would happen quickly, so I tried to get a bit of a head start on all the packing without feeling rushed.

I could have hired a company to handle it, but I knew that I needed to be the one to do it. To box up our things. To look at them one last time before saying good-bye. To let go of the memories I had assumed would be a part of our forever. I hoped it would be cathartic, sorting through our shared life and putting it into separate boxes. It was representative of the way the two of us existed now—once inseparable, now apart.

To be honest, it wasn't as hard as I'd imagined it would be. Maybe because I had taken a page from that Marie lady's playbook and thanked each one of Ryson's items before I placed it in a box, never to see it again. *Who knew that thanking things could help you let go of them? That Marie chick was really onto something.*

Taping up a box of Ryson's clothes from the closet, I was startled by a knock on the door. I narrowed my eyes, wondering who it could be. I knew that Madison and Paige were both at some showcase in the valley, and no one else aside from their boyfriends' knew the code to get past the gate. Curious, I walked down the long hallway.

Another knock.

Another.

It was the third knock that racked me with nerves. Someone on the other side was antsy, and it made me feel like they didn't belong at my front door. It would be easy to hop over the rod iron fence outside if you were determined enough. *Were they hoping I wasn't home, so they could rob the place? Maybe they'd heard I was thinking about selling?*

"Quinn!"

It was Ryson's voice, and it stopped me dead in my tracks. Even though I hadn't heard him say my name in months, the familiar tone and timbre caused time to stand still. My heart leaped inside my chest. It wanted out. Peeking through the peephole, I noticed him pacing back and forth. When he lifted his arm to knock again, I slowly opened the door, unsure of why he was here.

"Quinn," he breathed out, relief flooding his features as confusion flooded mine.

"What are you doing here?" I looked around his back to see how he'd gotten here.

I noticed his mom's Audi, but she wasn't in the driver's seat. *He'd driven himself?*

"I came to tell you something," he said, his voice coming out a mile a minute. "I mean, I have something to tell you."

"So, tell me," I started to say before my words were cut off by Ryson's lips pressing against mine.

My mouth opened without prodding, my tongue finding his like it had been made to do it. My brain spun, but I shut it up, forcing myself to get lost in the kiss, the feel of him, so familiar yet it had been so long. This man was my home, and every ounce of me recognized it. Part of me thought I should push him away and ask questions, but the rest of me screamed out to let this moment last for as long as he allowed it. Maybe I'd never get the chance again.

God, I'd missed him so much. Much more than I had ever allowed myself to realize until the moment his lips found mine. Only once Ryson pulled away did I find my footing, reaching out for the handrail to steady myself.

"I'm so sorry, Quinn. God, baby, I'm so sorry." Ryson looked pained as he cupped my cheek.

"Baby?" I asked, unsure of whether or not that word meant what I thought it meant. "You remember?" My eyes instantly welled with tears as something resembling hope filled my chest.

"I remember. I remember everything. I'm so damn sorry it took me so long," he announced before reaching for me again, his fingers tangling in my updo, his lips claiming mine. "I'm never going to stop kissing you," he breathed into me, and I found myself crying more than I was actually kissing him back.

He was the one to pull away again, breaking our mouths apart as we walked into the house, and he closed the door behind us. I was thankful the paparazzi had stopped camping out. Our story, while still newsworthy, wasn't what front pages were made of. At least, not anymore.

I realized that was all about to change … *again.*

"All I want to do is take you to the bedroom and make love to you until my body gives out, but we should probably talk first," Ryson said with a grin.

I smiled back, suddenly lost in the fantasy of Ryson's touch. A touch I'd thought I was never going to get to feel again.

"Well, that's a shame," I teased, "but you're probably right."

I couldn't believe that I was looking into the eyes that remembered me. I'd convinced myself that Ryson was lost to me forever, and now, here he was, home again.

"Talk first. Worship every single inch of you after," Ryson said.

I swore, my panties melted right off my body then and there.

This man.

I closed my mouth shut, forcing the thoughts from my mind, and tried to refocus as his hands continued to touch mine, almost like he was afraid to let go. And to be fair, maybe he was. The feel of his skin on my own was overwhelming.

"So, how did you remember? What happened? I want every detail," I asked as I led us into his office, his fingers wrapped in the belt loop of my shorts so I couldn't get away.

I wasn't sure why I'd picked that room in particular, but maybe it was because it was the only room I hadn't started packing yet. I thought I'd always knew that I'd get to it last. That his office would somehow be the most difficult to put into boxes and return to him. To be honest, I had barely walked in this room since the accident. But now that Ryson was here, I could go in it again and not want to throw up.

Looking around, I wasn't sure where to sit. As if reading

my mind, Ryson grabbed me. He sat down in the office chair and pulled me onto his lap, one hand tightly holding my back while the other pulled my hair out of the bun it had been in.

"My mom made me watch our movie." He gave me a crooked smile before kissing my neck. "She yelled at me. Told me she'd handcuff me to the chair if I didn't sit down and watch it," he explained between kisses.

Instead of laughing at what his mom had said, I rolled my eyes back in my head as a breathy moan escaped.

"Is this a dream?" I wasn't sure if I'd said it out loud or thought it in my head.

"Not a dream," Ryson answered between kisses, and I tried to move away from the spell he had me under, but his grip was too strong. "I'll stop. For now. Just don't leave." He sounded so worried, so unsure.

"Where would I go?" I looked into his dark eyes and cupped his face, still in disbelief that this was really happening. And when he didn't answer my question, I brought us back on point. "Is that really how it happened? You just watched our movie, and it all came rushing back?"

He offered me a shrug. "No, not exactly. I remembered some of my internal thoughts at first, but I wasn't sure what they were. I started talking to my mom about what I was seeing, and then more and more scenes started playing out in my head. I realized that they were memories. Of you. Of us. Once I made that realization, it was like someone flipped a switch in my head. I got it all back."

"I can't believe that. During our movie," I said, shaking my head.

I couldn't help but wonder if we could have saved our-selves a lot of time and heartache if we'd forced him to watch it months ago. I guessed we'd never know.

"Like I said, my mom insisted. I think it was her last-ditch effort. If that hadn't worked, she would have finally accepted that nothing was going to."

"I know the feeling."

"I came straight here. Once I remembered it all, I came right over to apologize, hoping like hell you'd forgive me."

Tears spilled down my cheeks. "Forgive you? It wasn't your fault."

His arms tightened around my back as he pulled me against him, his face burying in the crook of my neck. Warm tears spilled down my back, and I knew that my big, strong man was crying. It almost broke me apart.

"I know it wasn't my fault, Quinn, but I'll never forgive myself for not knowing who you were." He slowly pulled his head up, his dark eyes boring into mine, begging me for understanding. "How could I ever forget you? How could my heart and soul not know who you are? How, Quinn?"

Ryson and I had made a pact long ago to always be hon-est and tell each other the truth, no matter what. This could not be an exception to that particular rule.

Pushing out of his lap, I started full-on crying then, the tears rolling down my cheeks like someone had turned on a faucet. I paced back and forth in the room, a million feelings racing through me. Everything had caught up to me in that moment with his questions, all of my emotions warring against one another.

"I don't know. I asked myself that every day. I didn't want to be, but I was so mad at you. So mad and so hurt. I didn't understand how you could look at me and see nothing. You were so cold," I said as I stopped pacing, thankful that I didn't have to tiptoe around my feelings and worry about hurting his.

"I know I was. But I hated myself. It was the worst feeling, not knowing anything, but now that I'm back, I hate even more that I hurt you. I hate that I could ever talk to you the way that I did. I wasn't myself. I'm so sorry I left you. Please forgive me, Quinn. I'll never leave you again." He moved from the chair before falling to his knees and gripping the lower half of my body with all his might.

He was both begging for my forgiveness and offering himself up to me. Ryson was on his knees, letting me see that he belonged to me. Something I would never have questioned before the accident.

This was my man. My other half. My soul mate.

And it was what I'd been waiting for since the moment he first opened his eyes in the hospital. I'd wanted Ryson to come back to me for so long, but now that he was here, I felt conflicted. The majority of me was ecstatic to have him home; this was a literal dream come true. But there were small parts that longed for him to understand just how badly he'd hurt me in the process. As those thoughts entered my mind, I wondered just how truly fucked up I had become.

He sensed my hesitation. This man knew me better than anyone else. He could read me like a book.

"What is it?" He loosened his grip on me and rose to his

feet.

"I just …" I tried to figured out how to say it, but words failed me.

"You just what? You don't want me anymore?" Ryson took a few uneven steps back, his fingers running through his dark hair.

It was me who chased him this time, my arms wrapping around his waist. "Are you insane? Of course I want you. Don't ever question that. I am yours. I belong to you. I just need a minute."

"You need a minute? Why? What do you need a minute for, Quinn? Please help me understand because from what I see, we've wasted too many of those already."

"I know. But I can't just snap my fingers and make all the hurt from the past few months go away. I can't forget that easily."

Any girl in her right mind would throw everything out the window the second he walked back through the door. Only I would get so tangled up in my feelings that I would need a minute to untangle them. What the hell was wrong with me?

"I'm not asking you to forget. I'm asking you to work through it with me. Talk to me about it. Show me. Help me understand."

When he asked for that, something clicked inside me. "I did do a little writing," I said, referencing the folder on my computer that was filled with my emotional rantings.

"You journaled?" he asked, his eyes a little brighter than they had been a second ago.

I nodded. "Well, it's more like emotional vomit all over the page, but sure, we can call it journaling."

He laughed. "Can I read it?"

"Do you want to?" I got incredibly nervous.

I had tried once to read an entry after I wrote it, but my stomach had twisted into knots so tight, I thought they'd never unravel. I could literally *feel* my pain radiating off the page. They hurt way too badly for me to read, and I wondered how Ryson would take them.

"I think it might help," he said, sounding more like his mom than I'd ever heard before. "So I can see what you went through. So I can understand what it was like for you. Really like," he pushed.

"Okay," I agreed because I did not keep secrets from him. "I'll print them out. I don't know how many there are."

"It doesn't matter. Show me your heart, Quinn. Show me where I broke you," he pleaded.

I knew that letting him read what I'd been through in his absence was the right thing for us. Otherwise, it would live between us, this small chasm of distance in my heart that he could never reach and we could never repair.

"The writing was your mom's idea. By way of Paige, but still, it came from her."

He smiled, his head nodding. "Of course it was. She did the same thing to me."

"Did you journal too?" I asked through my curiosity.

His face turned ashy in color as he looked away. "Yeah. But trust me when I tell you that you don't want to read them." He sounded embarrassed.

"If they're anything like you were, I can imagine," I said, trying not to have hurt feelings over something seemingly so insignificant. "I'll be right back," I said, and the worried look returned to his eyes. "I'm just going to go print them. My laptop is in our bedroom."

"Okay." Ryson took a step toward me and touched my face like it was the first time. "I missed you so much," he said before kissing me like I held his heart in my hand.

"You have no idea how much I missed you. But you're about to." I gave him a grin before heading toward our bedroom to print out my heart, as he had called it. I hoped he could stomach reading them better than I could.

READING HER HEART
Ryson

AFTER QUINN LEFT to print out the pages to her heart, I walked over to my desk and pulled open the bottom right drawer. There was a small switch installed in the back, and when it was clicked, a secret door would spring open. I hadn't tested it in years and was thankful to see it still worked. It was brilliant, that little space, and was the whole reason I'd bought the antique piece in the first place. I'd thought it was cool, even if I hadn't known exactly what I'd be hiding in it.

On the drive over here, I'd made a phone call to a jeweler friend of mine and asked him to work on a rush order. Quinn had left me enough hints over the years that I knew exactly what kind of ring she wanted without even having to think about it. My girl might have been complicated and complex in every other way, but when it came to jewelry, she couldn't have been more classically simple. A round solitaire set in white gold was her dream ring.

That was it.

I almost hated getting her what she wanted because it

didn't seem special enough. If it had been up to me, I would have had something designed. It would have been over the top and elaborate with details hidden in the band and under the center stone. The ring would have been a reflection of the way I saw Quinn—unique, one of a kind, and gorgeous.

Yes, I planned on proposing. She was lucky I hadn't dropped to one knee the second she opened the front door. And trust me, I'd considered it.

After everything that had happened to me, it felt like the only thing in the world that mattered anymore was making her my wife. I wanted it just as much as she always had. The loss of my memory—and what had felt like my mind at times—was a pretty brutal reality check.

Once I'd remembered everything and put the pieces back together, I had been forced to take stock of what I really valued and held dear. That level of emotional upheaval had brought on heightened emotions I wouldn't have otherwise experienced. I couldn't have felt them, not to that extent, without the catalyst. I hated that it had taken something *that* dramatic and painful to force me to take a good, hard look at my life and see exactly where fear had ruled it, but it was the truth. For some idiotic reason, I had convinced myself over the years that if Quinn ever left me, it would hurt way less if we weren't married. Losing a girlfriend was one thing, but losing a wife had seemed like a whole different ball of wax.

Before the accident, I'd allowed myself to be controlled by this fear of loss, and I'd buried it under a myriad of bullshit excuses. Excuses that I'd actually believed at the time and convinced anyone who would listen to believe as well. But none of that mattered now. The old fears, the what-ifs—they were old news. I knew I had a lot of making up to do to Quinn, but I'd do whatever it took, for however long she needed.

Closing the door on my hidden compartment, I headed out of my office, dying to see the backyard. It was crazy how much I loved and had missed this house. As I walked out, I accidentally kicked something, and I looked down to see a box with my name written on it in black Sharpie. That was when I noticed the rest of the boxes scattered throughout the house. Quinn had been packing when I got here.

I ran my fingers across the top of the taped-up box just as Quinn rounded the corner. "Did you sell our house?"

She stopped short, a stack of papers in her hand. "No. Not yet. I was just trying to pack everything before I put it on the market."

"Do not sell our home, Quinn." I pulled at the tape until it loosened. Gripping it between my fingers, I ripped it clean off. I emptied the contents of the box on the ground in a heap before I headed to the next one to do the same. Our things did not belong in boxes.

"Ryson, stop," she said, but I wasn't having it.

"No. This is our home."

"That's exactly why I couldn't stay," she said, her tone so damn sad that it nearly crushed my heart.

I faced her, wanting to take her in my arms and never let go. "But I'm back now. And I'm never leaving again. So, you're either going to help me unpack all this shit or I'll do it myself," I threatened as I pulled at another piece of tape.

"Oh my gosh, I'll help. You're so impatient." She narrowed her eyes at me, and it felt like no time had passed.

"I've been here for an hour, and I haven't tasted every inch of you yet."

"Your point?" she asked as her cheeks pinked.

"My point is that if they were giving out trophies for patience, I'd win first place."

My God, I wanted this woman more than anything right now, but I knew that we needed to wait. Sex with Quinn was different. I'd convinced myself that most other couples did not have what we had between us. Sex had always bonded us, created a layer of intimacy that bordered on spiritual. I wanted to be inside her, but I needed to get inside her mind and heart first.

Before I reclaimed her body, I needed to see how badly I'd broken the rest of her.

Quinn plopped down on the floor, put the papers neatly on the ground in front of her, and started picking up the clothes I'd scattered. "I guess it's a good thing I'm a slow packer," she groaned.

I dropped down behind her and scooted her body between my legs. I'd never known how viscerally you could miss someone's smell until this moment. I buried my nose in her hair, breathing her in.

"Are you … sniffing me?" she asked with a giggle.

"Maybe," I said before breathing her in again.

"I used to grab your deodorant and smell it. And I might have refused to wash some of your shirts that still smelled like you," she admitted, and it was the cutest damn thing.

"You didn't wash my clothes?" I pretended to be grossed out.

She turned to swat my arm. "Just your shirts. I would wear them to sleep, but then they started to smell like me instead of you. And the last thing I needed was more stuff that smelled like me when I was running out of things that smelled like you."

Man, if her words were any indication of what I had waiting for me on those papers, I was in big trouble. They were going to break me in two.

"Hey, listen. I don't want to go, but—" I started to say.

She immediately turned around in my lap to face me. "But what? I just scared you off with the whole *never washing your clothes again* thing?"

I smiled and leaned down, pressing my lips against hers. "Hell no. Nothing you do could ever scare me off. It's just that I took my mom's car, and I need to get it back to her."

"Oh, yeah. I forgot. Do you want me to follow you there and bring you back here?" she asked, and just like that, we were finding our footing.

"Not yet," I said, and she looked a little crestfallen. "It's not what you think." I tried to comfort her and explain, "I want to read those first." I pointed at the stack of papers on the floor. "And I think it's better if I don't read them in front of you."

"Okay," she said almost nervously before blowing out a quick breath. "I think that's a good idea. That way, you can process them without me staring at you the whole time, asking you what you think."

I found myself laughing. "Yeah. And I'm not sure how much I want to cry in front of you. I know you think I'm super manly and tough, but you'd never be able to unsee me weeping like a baby."

Her expression turned instantly serious. "You joke, but I think you actually might cry."

"I'm not joking. I know I'm going to cry," I said, equally as serious. I also knew the guilt was going to eat away at me.

"Well then, I'd better let you get to your weep-fest."

I pushed to my feet and held out my hands. Pulling Quinn up, I tugged her straight into my chest and held her close. I could feel her heart beating against me. "I love you."

Her hazel eyes shone as she looked up at me. "I love you too. I hope you still love me after you read all those." She glanced at the floor.

I knew those papers were only going to make me love her more. "I'll call you."

"Okay."

Walking to the front door with her, hand in hand, I looked back at the entryway. "I'd start unpacking those unless you want to do it my way when I get back."

"Go." She stood on her toes and kissed me. "But hurry home."

Driving away from our house was weird. It wasn't natural. But I promised myself, even if I hadn't said it out loud to Quinn, I'd give her a little time to process the fact that I was back. I was a selfish prick though because I only planned on giving her this one night. Tomorrow, I was going to show up at our house and never leave again.

She could try to kick me out, but I knew she wouldn't.

When I got back to my mom's house, she was in the kitchen, drinking her favorite herbal tea. I filled her in on everything that had happened with Quinn, and she practically shoved me in my bedroom. I knew she would have locked it from the outside if she could have.

"I'm proud of you. For being so levelheaded about this and wanting to read the things she wrote. I'm sure it won't be easy. I'm here if you need me."

The sound of her feet shuffling echoed down the hall and away from my room as I reached for the first paper on top of the stack. I'd almost pulled over on the side of the road on my way back to my mom's, but I had known that once I started reading, I'd never be able to stop. I was grateful for that instinctual foresight. I couldn't imagine trying to read any of this in the car.

If I had thought for one second that I was in any way equipped for the onslaught of emotions that Quinn had felt during our time apart, I was dead wrong. Nothing could have prepared me for this. Her thoughts were honest, raw, and incredibly painful to read.

I feel like he's dead. And I find myself wondering if it would have been easier somehow if he had died. No, that's too fucked up. I take it back. I'm sorry, God. I don't mean it. Please don't take him even further away. I'm just so lost right now. Hurting so badly. The pain feels almost unbearable. Each breath hurts. All it does is remind me that I'm awake, alive, and filled with love for someone who no longer loves me back.

How is this possible? Why is this happening? And why is it happening to us? Were we too happy? Too good together? Did the Karmic scales need to be balanced somehow? Did one of us have to pay the price for some greater good? I don't know, but I want to. I want to know why. Why, why, why? I ask it constantly. And then I snap out of feeling sorry for myself because the answers never come. And they never will.

I just ... hurt so bad. And I know I keep saying it, but it's how I feel. I'm filled with so much pain, grief, and loss. I'm devastated. He isn't here anymore. But he still is. And that's so hard to wrap my head around—the fact that there is a complete and total absence of Ryson's presence even though he is still physically present.

What am I supposed to do? Just pretend this is all okay when it's the complete opposite of that? I can't believe he doesn't remember me. Doesn't remember us. How can he look at me and see nothing there? I still see my whole world every time I look at him. There's no way that will ever change. I'll never be able to look at him and feel nothing. I feel too much.

I can barely stand to be in this house without him. I hate sleeping in our bed. I hate everything right now. I hate this fucking journal, the thoughts in my head and my heart. I hate it all. I just want this all to be a bad dream.

I could hear her voice as I read each sentence, her emotions radiating through the pages. If her words were a heart, they would beat right through the paper, tearing it apart before breaking into pieces. Reading how badly I'd hurt her day after day stole the breath from my lungs.

I'd put my girl through total hell. And she'd lived there alone. Then again, you couldn't throw someone in the fire and expect them not to burn.

BACK HOME
Quinn

RYSON HADN'T SAID much when he left, so I had no idea when he planned on coming back. *What if reading my innermost thoughts made him stay away longer? What if my emotions were too heavy and he didn't want to shoulder them?* I was paranoid and worried. Two feelings I'd rarely, if ever, felt during the course of our relationship. It sucked.

I hadn't even called Paige or Madison to let them know that Ryson was back. I'd decided not to call anyone. At least not without talking to Ryson first. I probably should let people know that he was back, but it still felt so new and a little uncertain. *What if Ryson woke up tomorrow and didn't remember again? What if his memories didn't stay?* I knew I couldn't go through it all a second time, and I refused to put anyone else through it either until we knew for sure that he was back for good.

Looking around at the boxes that Ryson had pulled the tape from, I started laughing. He could be such a brat sometimes, but that was part of what I loved about him. I couldn't believe he had been here. Ryson had touched me, kissed me, told me he loved me. When I'd decided it was time to move on with my life, I'd truly accepted that none of those things would ever happen again.

I'd never been happier to be wrong in my entire existence. It felt like a dream, so I pinched myself to make sure I was awake and then yelled at myself for squeezing so hard. I kicked a few boxes down the hall toward our bedroom, so I could unpack them.

Am I supposed to unthank the clothes for their service now that they're staying? I wondered. That Marie chick didn't have any lessons in her teachings for this kind of thing.

I shrugged to myself and decided I'd welcome them back home as I hung them in place.

My cell phone pinged, and my whole body sprang to life. Hope and giddiness made the butterflies swarm in my stomach, and I felt myself smiling before I even knew who the text message was from.

RYSON: I JUST WANTED YOU TO KNOW HOW MUCH I MISS YOU, AND I CAN'T STAND BEING APART. I DON'T WANT TO BE HERE WITHOUT YOU. IT FEELS LIKE WE'RE WASTING PRECIOUS TIME.

ME: COME HOME.

I didn't have to overthink or overanalyze when it came to how I felt about him. I sent that response because it was what I wanted, what I needed. I was sure it might have been smarter to give ourselves a little distance, like he had suggested, but you try losing the love of your life and then staying away from him when he finally came to his senses.

Literally.

It wasn't as easy as you would think to be rational or logical. My emotions were the ones in control. I paced the hallway as I waited for him to get here. I checked my reflection in the mirror a thousand times, knowing that Ryson couldn't care less how I looked, but I still wanted to feel cute.

The front door finally opened, and I was thankful he didn't knock like he had earlier.

I practically sprinted into his arms, my lips finding his as I thanked him for coming back home to me. "What took you so long?"

"I had to call for a ride."

"Oh. Yeah," I said, feeling dumb because his car was still here in the garage.

"I wasn't going to come until tomorrow, but I couldn't wait. I'm sorry. I know I told you I'd give you time—" he apologized.

I silenced him with another kiss because, sometimes, my boyfriend was dumb.

"I'm glad you didn't." I had been missing him terribly since he walked out the door. "What's all this?" I pointed to the box he held in his hand that was overflowing with papers and notebooks.

He grinned. "I read your journals. Come on," he said before giving me a slight nod and reaching for my hand. Our fingers intertwined, and he pulled me into the kitchen and dropped the box onto the table.

"What did you think?" I asked with a slight wince.

"They were devastating." His eyes met mine, and the

pain my words had caused him was written all over his face. "I don't even know how to apologize for putting you through that. Saying sorry doesn't seem like enough."

I didn't want to keep punishing him for something he'd had no control over. Yes, I'd been damaged, but I wasn't beyond repair. Not anymore.

"It wasn't your fault."

Ryson didn't accept that reasoning; I could tell.

"But it was. I just ..." He paused, the pain on his face causing a physical reaction of my own. "I feel so guilty. I hurt you in the worst way. Even if you forgive me, how can I ever forgive myself?"

I reached across the table, taking his hand in mine and squeezing. It was a simple gesture, but I could tell that he needed it. My touch, my acceptance, and my understanding—they were all vital for him to truly heal. It made perfect sense to me because I required the exact same things from him too.

"You will forgive yourself because you weren't yourself. I called you New Ryson and Old Ryson. We all did. Because it was so clear that who you became was not who you once had been."

His eyes started to water, and there was something about his vulnerability that made him even sexier in my eyes. "I must have been really great in a past life to deserve you in this one," he said with a weak smile.

"I'm not going to pretend like it was rainbows and roses and a super-easy thing to go through"—I pointed at the printed sheets—"because we both know that'd be a lie."

"Is this supposed to make me feel better?" he asked as he wiped at his eye with the back of his hand.

I shot him a look that told him I wasn't finished. "I had to adjust to a whole new life. A life I had never planned for and definitely didn't want. But none of that matters now because you're back. And all I want is you. You have no idea how many times I wished for this. Or how often I pleaded with God."

He reached for the sheets of paper and held them up in the air. "I have a pretty good idea."

"Are they that bad?"

"You wrote them. Don't you remember?" He laughed like it was the most ridiculous question.

"But I never read them. I couldn't."

His head nodded slowly. "I get that. They aren't easy reads."

We stayed quiet, looking into each other's eyes like it was the first time. Or like it might be the last. I knew that Ryson not only recognized me, but also loved me deeply, just from that look. And I swore, I'd never take it for granted again.

He blinked twice and sucked in a deep breath. "You're really beautiful, you know that?" Before I could respond or answer, he continued, "Sorry. That was off topic, but it needed to be said. Anyway, I brought these over because I had an idea." He pointed at the box.

"What is all that?"

"It's your journals and mine."

"You brought me your journals?" I asked, remembering

that he'd told me earlier I shouldn't read them.

"Yes, and no. I still don't think you should read them because they're pretty awful. But, of course, if you wanted to, I wouldn't stop you. It's just that New Ryson was pretty angry," he said.

I laughed at that. "Tell me about it." I rolled my eyes.

"I know. I'm sorry," he apologized for the fiftieth time.

"It's okay. Don't say you're sorry for that anymore. I know you feel bad, but I don't want you to keep feeling bad. Okay?"

He swallowed hard, his jaw flexing as if this was going to be a struggle. "Okay."

"Now, tell me what you did here." I pointed back to the table.

"So, I had this idea while I was reading your stuff. It made me think of the things I had written. So, I went through and started piecing together parts of mine with yours. Not all of it because I think I could have spent days getting it just right, and I wanted to come back."

"I'm glad you did. Now, what do you mean? You pieced them together how?" I reached for the stack he held out and flipped through them.

"On some of them, I used correlating dates. Your entry on a particular day, followed by mine on the same day, or vice versa. That was easy. But on others, I started including your thoughts, and then I inserted things that I had written on the same subject. It's actually pretty fascinating from a psychological standpoint."

"You are definitely your mother's son." I shook my head

but couldn't disagree. It was intriguing to say the least.

Reading our thoughts side by side was tear-jerking, to say the least. Everything I had written was so singularly focused on losing Ryson. And Ryson talked about how he couldn't remember what he'd lost because, from his perspective, he'd lost every-damn-thing.

His entries made me sad. And for the first time, I understood what it must have really been like for him to not remember anything or anyone from his life. The way he'd described feeling lost pulled at my heart. The pressure he'd felt from me and the disappointment I'd made him feel over and over again was heart-wrenching to read.

"This would make an amazing book," I said, not believing my own ears. *Hadn't I just adamantly told Paige that I'd never sell or publish my private thoughts?*

"I was thinking the same thing. That's kind of why I organized it that way. Does it read like a novel?"

"It reads like a story I wouldn't wish on my worst enemy," I said, and he smirked. *God, how I'd missed that smirk.* "But it's actually pretty captivating."

"I knew you'd think so. We should talk to Madison about shopping around for a publishing deal. Or maybe we could publish it ourselves and keep all the creative and editorial control? Not to mention, the pricing and promotions. We could come up with a killer marketing plan to tie into the reality show too." And, literally, just like that, Old Ryson was back, his mind spinning and working the way it always had. "Wait. Do our friends know that I'm back?"

"No. It didn't seem right to tell them without you."

"My partner in crime," he said before adding, "We really should call Madison though."

"Why? The book idea can wait."

"Not for the book. I want to make a statement," he said casually. "And I want to schedule it soon."

"What kind of statement?" I asked as scenes of chaos filled my mind. "I feel like I just got rid of the paparazzi. Trust me, the last thing we need is them back on our doorstep. They stayed for weeks."

His head crooked to the side as softness filled his features. "Quinn, you had to go on TV and tell the whole world that I didn't want to be with you anymore."

I visibly cringed with his words as the memory played in my mind.

"I want to go on TV and make sure the whole world knows that I do."

I felt any worries I'd had fade away as my tension eased. "Ryson, you are the most thoughtful man, but I don't need that."

"But—"

"No buts," I interrupted. "I promise, I don't need that from you. I just need this." I reached across the table and grabbed a fistful of his shirt, tugging his lips down to mine.

I knew that Ryson loved me. I didn't need him proclaiming it to the world. His actions had always spoken louder than any words ever could.

"I know you're sorry for all you put me through, but it wasn't intentional. I don't need you to make some grand gesture to the public. All I need is you here, with me."

"Are you sure?"

"I'm more than sure."

"Fine." He wasn't fully on board with this, but I'd get him there. "No statement. But let's make sure we call everyone tomorrow and invite them over. Don't tell them why. We'll surprise them. And then I can talk to Madison about the book and get her take on signing with a publisher versus self-publishing."

I'd forgotten how much I loved the way his mind worked. How much I respected the way he could take the smallest idea and turn it into three or four different avenues for success.

"You never stop creating."

"Well, to be fair, I took a break there for a little bit. I have a lot of catching up to do."

He gave me a quick shrug, and I laughed.

"Well, to be fair," I said, mimicking his words, "that's not the only thing you need to catch up on." I pushed back from the chair and wagged my finger at him before taking off, running down the hall, knowing damn well he'd catch me just like I wanted him to.

I MISSED MY LIFE
Ryson

WHERE THE HELL *was she hiding?* No sooner had I asked myself that stupid question when the water for the shower turned on. Like a lightbulb over my head, I headed into the bathroom to find my woman in there, moving to get herself undressed.

"Hey. That's my job." I reached for her arm, stopping her. "Let me."

It had been too long since I saw her this way. Too long since I touched her. Too long since she belonged to me in every way.

I removed her clothes, one torturous item at a time, when all I really wanted to do was rip them to shreds with my bare teeth. Quinn stood quietly in front of me, completely exposed, and she had never looked more beautiful. Kissing her neck, I wrapped my arms around her waist, my fingers brushing the top of her ass. She really did have the best ass—and not because it'd kept winning online awards, but because it was mine.

"My turn," she whispered against my chest as she moved

to remove any article of clothing that covered me. "I have missed you"—she sucked in a breath—"missed this, so much."

"Me too," I said as I stood there, watching her watching me.

She reached for my hand and led me into our shower. It felt like years since I'd stepped foot in here. There were new bottles of shampoo, and my stuff was missing. I looked around like it was brand-new, and I guessed, in a way, it sort of was.

"I packed your shower stuff away. I'm sorry. It hurt me to see them every time I came in here." She faced me, the water hitting her back.

"You don't have to apologize either, Quinn. Not for the things you had to do to survive. I understand. And even though there is nothing to forgive, I forgive you too. For whatever you think needs to be forgiven." I kissed the top of her head before I pivoted her body around, her back against my front.

I instantly hardened, but I refused to fuck Quinn for the first time in the damn shower. I wondered how quickly I could get us out as I reached for her shampoo. Squeezing it into my hand, I worked it into a lather in her hair. She moaned. She. Literally. Fucking. Moaned.

"Quinn," I warned as I hardened even more. "Stop making those sounds, or I'm taking you to bed, covered in soap."

"Then, stop washing my hair so slow. Get us out of here already."

She turned to face me, and I could see the lust in her

eyes. She had missed our connection as much as I had. Probably more since she wasn't the one who had lost her mind.

"Glad we're on the same page," I said before dunking her head in the water.

"Ryson!" She laughed.

"Just get out. We can shower after. Why the hell did we start in here in the first place?"

"I'd been packing all day. I was gross."

She bent over dramatically and unnecessarily to turn off the water, and I damn near exploded.

"Out. Get out," I demanded.

She stood upright in painfully slow movements. She knew exactly what she was doing to me, and she enjoyed every second of it.

"I do remember something about a promise." She stepped out of the shower, wrapping her body tightly in a towel the way women knew how to do.

I pulled the towel free and threw it to the ground. "No towel. What promise?"

"I distinctly recall you saying something about *tasting every inch of me*. Or maybe that offer expired?" she teased.

I nipped at her neck before taking her mouth with mine and claiming it like she was the last drop of water on the planet and I was a dying, dehydrated man.

"I'm afraid I might not last very long." I walked her over toward the bed until we reached the edge of it.

"I don't care. I need to be with you," she said the words with such sincerity that I knew she meant them.

Quinn belonged to me, and I belonged to her. I wasn't naive enough to think that we wouldn't have some issues to work through, but I was confident enough to know that we could get through anything as long as we were together. I planned on locking Quinn down, making her my wife, and never letting her go again, if she'd have me.

"Stop stalling," she said, breaking me from my trance.

"I think you've gotten even bossier since I was away," I said before licking and biting at her bare skin.

"Guess you'll have to find out." She dug her nails into my back and pulled at me with her fingertips.

"Oh, I plan on it. I plan on finding out all night."

"Less talk. More action."

"You belong to me, Quinn. I think you might have forgotten," I growled.

She bit her bottom lip in response, daring me. "So remind me," she said, and I reached between her thighs, my entire body swelling at how ready she was for me.

I planned on reminding my girl over and over again until the sun came up. Maybe even longer. As I looked down at her beautiful face, her hazel eyes looking up at me with so much hope, love, and desire, I knew that we were going to be okay.

And as soon as I picked up her ring, we were going to be even better.

EPILOGUE

ONE MONTH LATER
REALITY SHOW FILMING—DAY ONE

Quinn

THE CAMERAS WERE set up inside our house and in the backyard, and our entire friend group was here for the first day of filming, getting their mics attached to their bodies. I currently had one taped between my boobs and a battery pack around my waist, pulling down my shorts with each step I took. It was awkward, but I had been told I'd get used to it. Shooting the first episode here at our home couldn't have been more perfect. It felt right to start filming where we'd all agreed to do this project in the first place.

The reality show had been green-lit the minute Ryson told the network he was ready. Howard had signed on to produce the show, like he'd promised, but was out of the country for our first few filming dates. He assured us all that he didn't need to be on set for every shoot and most likely wouldn't. His role was more to oversee the footage after the fact, step in when necessary, offer creative changes, worry about the budget, and keep the network happy. When he'd told Ryson that he trusted the show in his hands, I swore, my man had almost passed out.

Once the news had broken that Ryson had his memory back, everyone wanted a piece of him, a piece of us. We turned down all offers for on-camera and online interviews, which only made everyone want us even more. Ryson and I had known that would happen, but we stayed a stoically silent, a united front in preparation for our surprise book release. It only took two phone calls with Madison to decide that we wanted to publish the book on our own terms and have complete editorial control. It felt like the right decision.

I'd been struck with a very personal realization one afternoon when it came to myself, Ryson, and our celebrity status. For whatever reason, I'd always felt somewhat indebted to the public, like they deserved all the credit for my fame and success because they were always so supportive of it. But my success wasn't because of the fans. And going through what I had with Ryson changed my perspective on the matter.

I no longer felt obligated to fill in every missing piece so that their curiosity was satisfied and they felt included. And while I still wanted to share personal things with them, I wanted to be the one in charge of what those things were. The book and the reality show were the beginning of seeing those hopes come to life.

Ryson and I continued to have mostly good days. A few bad ones crept in every now and then. Either I would remember what it had been like to be without him or he would be so guilt-ridden for the way he'd treated me that he couldn't even look me in the eyes. We were works in progress on that front, but that was what traumatic events did to people. They didn't leave you unscarred or unscathed. You fought to come out the other side, and when you did, it was with battle wounds that bled when you least expected them to. I thought the hardest part for us was accepting that even having these wounds to begin with was normal and didn't mean that we were irreparably broken.

There was nothing too big that we couldn't get through as long as we were together. Even on days where we questioned everything else in the world, we never questioned that.

"Quinn!" Paige's voice shrieked.

I looked around before one of the crew pointed his finger in the direction of my shouting best friend.

"What's wrong?" I asked as soon as I found her, her face twisted into a scowl.

"Where am I supposed to put this?" She held out the microphone's battery pack like it disgusted her, and two crew members shrugged their shoulders at me. It wasn't like Paige to act so diva-esque.

"Under your dress. Stop acting like you're new to this."

"Sorry for shouting. I didn't want some strange guy to cop a feel," she admitted in a whisper.

I took the pack from her hands. "Well, I'm definitely copping one." I laughed as I reached under her dress to wrap the material around her middle.

"It's going to stick out all weird in the back. It's not like they're small," she complained.

I stopped myself from rolling my eyes. "Look, my shorts are going to fall off, but you don't hear me complaining." The equipment was heavy, and I kept subconsciously reaching for the waistband of my shorts and hiking them up.

"Remind me not to wear a dress again," she said, patting around her back until she reached the protruding equipment. "Can you tighten it?"

"I'll make a note," I said as I reassured her, reaching my hands back in. "I'm sure they'll film from the waist up. Or only from the front. They know what they're doing, and we're not trying to make anyone look bad."

"Uh, what's going on in here?" Tatum walked in, and I froze, my hands stilled. "You could have asked me to fondle you."

I pulled my hands out, and Paige turned to swat Tatum on the shoulder with a fake scowl.

"She wasn't fondling me. Why'd you let me wear a dress?"

Tatum looked between the two of us, clearly confused as he put both his hands in the air and slowly backed away.

"You know he has no idea why you can't wear a dress, right?" I asked before we both started laughing.

"Why are you two in here without me?" Madison appeared, looking sun-kissed and glowy.

"Why were you out there without us?" I fired back as I wrapped an arm around each girl, pulling them against my shoulders.

"Sometimes, I still can't believe we got Ryson back," Madison said, and I smiled to myself.

Sometimes, I couldn't believe it either, but then I would open my eyes and see him lying next to me in bed, and all would be right in the world.

"I feel so lucky that things worked out the way they did." I knew that it could have gone a very different way for me and Ryson. At one point, I'd accepted that it had. But I was beyond grateful that it hadn't.

"We all do." Paige sniffed.

I sucked in a loud breath before shoving my two best friends away. "No. We are not crying before we start filming. Makeup and hair will kill us. Ryson will kill us. Save the emotions for the cameras." I stepped away like they were contagious.

"Girls!" It was Ryson. "Get out here!"

"Guess that's our cue," I said before leading us into the backyard where the guys all stood, the camera crew surrounding them and waiting.

"We're ready to start," Ryson said, his face practically beaming with excitement as he chatted with the crew members, most likely giving direction. "Is everyone ready?" he asked as the couples moved toward one another, arms wrapping around waists, murmuring their okays.

We each ran through a quick mic check to test for levels and sound. When we got the thumbs-up, one of the crew members grabbed the scene marker and called out the information as the six of us stood around the built-in barbeque, trying to look natural. I almost started cracking up, but I knew that Ryson would kill me.

"Rolling. And action."

This was it. Filming had officially begun.

As I looked at Ryson, he dropped to one knee in front of me, and the rest of the world disappeared. *What the hell was he doing?*

He opened the box, and a sparkling solitaire diamond ring shone back at me. It was exactly the kind of ring I'd always wanted.

"Quinn, you are the love of my life. I put you through hell this past year, and if there's one thing I've learned, it's that I never want to go a day without you by my side." He reached for my left hand, his thumb rubbing the skin there as his eyes looked squarely into mine. "I used to think that you being my girlfriend was enough. That I didn't need the paperwork or the title to show you how much I loved you." His head shook like he was the world's biggest idiot. "But I was wrong. It's not enough," he said.

My eyes instantly started spilling the tears I'd been trying to hold back.

"I need you to be my wife. I was a fool for ever trying to convince myself otherwise. Marry me, Quinn. Never leave my side, and I'll never leave yours. I promise I'll always remember you, love you, and worship the ground you walk on. Until death parts us."

I couldn't believe what I was seeing, what I was hearing. And here I'd been, trying to convince myself that this wasn't something I needed anymore.

"Wait. Cut. End. Stop." I looked around at everyone before looking back down at Ryson kneeling before me. "Is this real? Or are you doing this for the camera? I mean, they literally just started rolling."

Ryson laughed before his face turned beet red. "You think I'd propose for a show? For ratings? You think I'd fake this?"

"I don't know! No! Of course not! I mean ..." I was stumbling and stuttering and making a fool of myself, and the cameras were still rolling; I sensed it. I started whispering, forgetting that I was mic'd up and they'd still hear whatever I said anyway. "Are you sure this is what you want? We don't have to get engaged. When I lost you, I realized that all I needed was you. I didn't care about the rest of it. I don't need anything else if you don't."

Why the heck was I trying to talk him out of proposing to me?

"Well, I do. I need it all. Every single ounce of you that you'll give me. Forever, Quinn," Ryson said my name softly, his thumb still rubbing circles on my hand. "Say yes. Wear this ring. Be my wife. Share my last name. But please say yes, so I can get up."

He laughed, and I laughed, reaching for his face.

"Yes! Of course, yes." I pulled at him.

His lips crashed into mine as my heart grew inside my chest. He slid the ring onto my finger as I continued kissing him, lost in the moment.

Between kisses, he asked, "Forever?"

"And then some," I answered.

Everyone started clapping. Or maybe they'd been clapping all along. I'd honestly forgotten they were there. It was funny how the world could disappear around you and you could lose all focus on everyone but one person.

I looked around, regaining my composure, and noticed that my parents were suddenly there in the backyard. So was Ryson's mom. *When had they arrived?*

"Did you all know he was going to do this?"

My girlfriends clamored to see my ring and hugged me.

"Hell yes, we knew," Tatum said.

"We were all in on it," Walker added.

"Us too," my parents said before wrapping me in a hug. "Congratulations, sweetie. We couldn't be happier for you both."

"I'm so thrilled you two found your way back to each other," Ryson's mom said, and I hugged her through my tears.

"When did you all find out? How long have you known?" I found myself wanting to know every detail.

How long had Ryson planned this? When had he bought the ring? When had his mind changed?

My dad cast a glance at Ryson before giving me what I wanted. "He came over and talked to us a few weeks ago. Apologized for everything that had happened and then asked for our permission. Showed us the ring and everything."

A few weeks ago? He'd just come back to me at that point.

"He already had the ring?" I asked.

My dad nodded through my shock. It wasn't that Ryson's actions were shocking exactly; it was more that I'd had no idea he'd bought a ring or gone over to see my parents. *When had he done all this, and where had I been when it hap-*

pened? Ryson and I had been practically inseparable since we reunited.

"I can't believe you asked my parents for their permission," I said as I looked at the ring and smiled. It was so beautiful, so perfect.

"Of course I did, babe. You think I'd ever ask you something like this without asking them first?" Ryson sounded almost offended.

My man was a gentleman. In every sense of the word. And he was all mine. And soon, the entire world was going to know it, and I couldn't be happier about that fact.

"You're going to be my husband!" I shouted before jumping into his arms.

Everyone started laughing and cheering. Madison walked out of the house, carrying two bottles of champagne, and my mom followed behind her with a bunch of flutes.

Mads handed the bottles to Walker, who popped them open with ease before he started pouring. Madison and Paige handed each of us a half-filled glass.

"A toast," Walker started. "To the couple we all look up to. You two are an inspiration to us all. Thank you for letting us be a part of your lives. We are so happy for you."

I cried. For so many reasons.

Like for the kind things that Walker had said. And the way my parents were currently beaming at us like they had never been prouder in their lives. I cried for the way Madison stood, sipping her champagne and typing away on her phone with the goofiest smile on her face, which meant she was most likely writing a press release about what had just happened. And for the way Tatum was looking at Paige, like he couldn't wait to do the exact same thing for her someday. And the way Paige was wrapped up in his arms, most likely thinking the same thing. And I cried for the way Ryson's mom stood there, watching us, her hand held over her heart like she couldn't be more delighted—until we gave her grandkids, I'd bet.

And for the man at my side, the man who would never leave it again. I cried because our story hadn't always been easy, but it was beautiful, even when it had been tragic. I wouldn't want our story to have ended any other way.

That was one statement I couldn't wait to make to the press.

THE END

Phew! Man, I sure hope you loved Ryson & Quinn's story as much as I did. What a roller coaster of emotions, huh? Have you read the other books in The Celebrity Series? They're FREE in Kindle Unlimited!

Seeing Stars—Madison & Walker
Breaking Stars—Paige & Tatum

I have a set of three brothers you have got to meet! I just know you're going to love them! The first book in the series is called *No Bad Days*, and it's FREE in Kindle Unlimited.

Or if you'd like to read a really fun enemies-to-lovers romance about rival wineries, read BITTER RIVALS! I know you're going to love it!

Thank you so much for reading and enjoying my stories. They are all free in Kindle Unlimited right now, so you should read them. It will be fun. LOL. But, seriously, thank you.

OTHER BOOKS BY J. STERLING

Bitter Rivals—An Enemies-to-Lovers Romance
Dear Heart, I Hate You—A Contemporary Romance
10 Years Later—A Second Chance Romance
In Dreams—New Adult College Romance
Chance Encounters—Coming-of-Age Story

The Game Series:
The Perfect Game—Book One
The Game Changer—Book Two
The Sweetest Game—Book Three
The Other Game (Dean Carter)—Book Four

The Playboy Serial:
Avoiding the Playboy—Episode #1
Resisting the Playboy—Episode #2
Wanting the Playboy—Episode #3

The Celebrity Series:
Seeing Stars—Madison & Walker
Breaking Stars—Paige & Tatum
Losing Stars—Quinn & Ryson

The Fisher Brothers Series:
No Bad Days—New Adult, Second Chance Romance
Guy Hater—Emotional Love Story
Adios Pantalones—Single Mom Romance
Happy Ending

ABOUT THE AUTHOR

Jenn Sterling is a Southern California native who loves writing stories from the heart. Every story she tells has pieces of her truth in it as well as her life experience. She has her bachelor's degree in radio/TV/film and has worked in the entertainment industry the majority of her life.

Jenn loves hearing from her readers and can be found online at:

Blog & Website:
www.j-sterling.com

Twitter:
twitter.com/AuthorJSterling

Facebook:
facebook.com/AuthorJSterling

Private Facebook Reader Group:
facebook.com/groups/ThePerfectGameChangerGroup/

Instagram:
instagram.com/AuthorJSterling

If you enjoyed this book, please consider writing a spoiler-free review on the site from which you purchased it. And thank you so much for helping me spread the word about my books and for allowing me to continue telling the stories I love to tell. I appreciate you so much. :)

Thank you for purchasing this book.

Please join my mailing list to get updates on new and upcoming releases, deals, bonus content, personal appearances, and other fun news!

tinyurl.com/pf6al6u